THE
SUPERNATURAL
SOCIETY

THE SUPERNATURAL SOCIETY

.sterces sah dik yrevE

.tey srieht wonk t'nod tsuj eerht esehT

REX OGLE

inkyard PRESS

Recycling programs for this product may not exist in your area.

ISBN-13: 978-1-335-42487-7

The Supernatural Society

This edition published by arrangement with Harlequin Books S.A.

For questions and comments about the quality of this book, please contact us at CustomerService@Harlequin.com.

Inkyard Press
22 Adelaide St. West, 41st Floor
Toronto, Ontario M5H 4E3, Canada
www.InkyardPress.com

Printed in U.S.A.

To Marisa.

…who died.

And has kept me company ever since.

THE
SUPERNATURAL
SOCIETY

a grave warning

To the human child reader reading this:

Rex Ogle is a liar. He did not write this book. I did. Rex wishes he were half the monster that I, your humble narrator, am. Why would someone wish to be a monster? I have no idea. But now that we have that bit of unpleasant business out of the way...

I beg of you—do NOT read this story.

Go on, then. Put this ~~cross~~ book down. It will not hurt my feelings. After all, I have had an awful and terrible life, and am certain that you would not want to read something that I worked so very hard to ~~out~~ write. My narrative here is likely to be ~~every~~ more grisly and ghastly than my grotesque face—which is more hideous than you can imagine.

You do not believe me? Then ~~other~~ understand this: when I was born, the nurse screamed and the doctor fainted. My mother took one look at me, scrunched up her face like she had tasted a sour lemon, and cried, "Oh, dear! It seems we have given birth to a terrible abomination." Soon after, my father abandoned me at the edge of a dark wood...

But never mind me. We are here to discuss a different ~~letter~~ story, the one you hold in ~~in~~ your hands at this very moment, the same one that I strongly recommend again and again that you NOT read.

Please, I beg of you: get rid of this book. Toss it into the trash. Or better yet, destroy it. Run it over with a bike, flush it down a toilet, or throw it off a tall mountain into a deep canyon. Better yet, douse it with lighter fluid and hurl it into the nearest fire—with adult supervision, of course. Fire is both ~~alphabetical~~ terrifying and dangerous.

Yes, do that. Go on. I will wait.

...

...

...

Why are you still here, holding this book? Stop reading this at once! I ~~order~~ demand it!

(Please?)

You are still reading, aren't you? For crying out loud! Fine. If I cannot appeal ~~to~~ to your heart, perhaps I can speak some sense into your brain. ~~Find~~ Here are three reasons to forget this book as soon as possible:

#1. Because I am a MONSTER. And everyone knows monsters are not writers–at least not good ones.

#2. Because this story is ~~my~~ a TRUE story. And true stories are boring. It is much better to read fiction–which are ~~secret~~ NOT true stories.

#3. Because the following chapters contain MONSTERS, MYTHS, MAGIC, and MAD SCIENCE–which means if you are not bored, then you will be upset, alarmed, scared, and frightened.

Do you want all that?

What do you mean, "YES"?! Of all the foolish and ridiculous...!

No, this is your ~~message~~ choice. And I support your choosing–even if I disagree with every fiber of my foul being. I guess there's no more arguing with you.

So instead I will BEG! Please please please please please please please please please please please please PLEASE (with poison on top), do NOT read this tale. It will bore you to tears, or intense laughter, or perhaps it will scare you... TO DEATH.

I see you are still reading. Fine. I am getting up off my knees. There is no use. You are incorrigible.

Oh, well. I did my best. You were warned. ~~Good luck~~.

Sincerely, and WORST,

yours darkly,

-Adam Monster

p.s.

Mayb sctdoerfyg ihsi fjiklllmendo wpiqtrhs steucvrwextysz,

Haïbdcddeenf ignh ciojdkelsm, cniopphqerrsst, aunvdw cxryyzpatbocgdreafmgsh.

Fiijnkdl tmhneomp aqlrls-itfu yvowux cyazna.

Chapter 1

The Fresh Start

✷

Will's life was over.

No, he was not dead—*yet*—but it felt like everything was ending. A feeling which threatened to suffocate him.

It was the second week of October when Will Hunter was forced to pack his entire life into cardboard boxes. His video games, his comic book collection, his soccer ball, the photos of friends he might never see again—all of it was going with him. Yet each time Will taped a box closed, he cringed, like someone had put another nail in his coffin.

On a sullen Sunday, he woke to find his mom had already packed the car and locked the trailer behind it. She said, "It's time to go."

"I don't want to," Will whined.

"I'm sorry, Will. We don't have any other choice."

Dear Reader, as you might imagine, these words made Will miserable. He hated not having a choice. You see, Will already felt powerless in many ways. He didn't get to choose how tall he was (more short than tall), the color of his skin (tan but easily browned by the sun), or how remarkable he was (not remarkable at all). And he hardly had a choice in his dad's departure or his mom's move. In sum, Will hated not having a choice.

As his mother drove, Will stared out the window with burning eyes. His arms were crossed across his chest, and had been since they left the state of New York. He did not want to leave home. He did not want to move to a new town. And he certainly did not want what his mother kept referring to as a "fresh start."

The car moved east along the interstate highway, the Long Island Sound just south of them. In between songs on the radio, Will's mom asked, "Are you ever going to speak to me again?"

"No," Will answered curtly.

The drive dipped in and out of small towns and big cities. As they passed gas stations and rest stops and too many trees to count, Will could think only one thing: *This sucks*. But what he really meant was, *I'll never make friends or have fun again. Especially not in a* boring dumb town *like wherever the heck we're going*.

Dear Reader, what Will didn't know—that I, your humble author, *do* know—is that he was very, very wrong. This town to which he was headed is many things—but boring is *not* one of them.

Before long they entered Massachusetts, and the car turned onto a road that had a single lane. As they drove north, then west, Will looked at the map on his mom's phone. The land appeared to spiral in on itself until it drowned in the ocean, like going down a toilet drain. They passed through Provincetown, then onto a bridge that stretched over the water for miles and miles. Waves floated back and forth, rolling over and over until they disappeared onto the horizon. Will considered how far they were from a real city—they were in the middle of nowhere, surrounded by water. Will realized he needed to learn how to swim.

WELCOME TO EAST EMERSON!

That was what the sign should have read. Instead, someone had scribbled out the first two words and replaced them. Now the sign said:

HOPE YOU SURVIVE
~~WELCOME TO~~ EAST EMERSON!

The sign was surrounded by giant dead trees whose branches hung down like skeleton arms. Goose bumps ran up Will's arms as the car crossed a bridge onto a small island containing an even smaller town.

"Did you see that sign?" Will asked.

His mom shrugged. "Probably teenagers having some fun. What they should have written was, 'This is a great place for a fresh start!'"

"More like the opposite," Will muttered.

As the car turned onto Main Street, Will's mom smiled and pointed. "Look—here's the town square. It has a beautiful green park, a gazebo, a statue of…is that an explorer riding a fish?"

Will rolled his eyes. "It's a Viking stabbing a serpent through the heart."

"Look over there," Mom continued. "A library, a post

office, a café, an antique store, even a little movie theater. How exciting!"

"New York City has like a million movie theaters," Will mumbled. East Emerson was full of faded signs and crumbling storefronts. Nothing was shiny or new like home. There wasn't a single skyscraper scraping the sky. Nothing was familiar. As far as Will was concerned, he might as well be on a different planet.

"Well, look at that cute little general store," his mom said. "They have funny Halloween masks in the window."

The masks at the bizarre shop were *not* funny—they were frightening. Some masks were vicious animal faces, others horrific human faces, and a lot were devilish devil faces. As the car drove past, the masks' eyes followed Will. More goose bumps rose, this time on the back of his neck.

"Such a beautiful town," his mom commented. "So much space. Can you smell the fresh ocean air?"

"Smells stupid," Will grumbled.

"Will, I know this is hard—" Mom started, but Will cut her off.

"Hard? Hard?! Math tests are hard. Moving to a strange new place is worse than hard—it's…it's…the suckiest thing in the history of sucky things!"

Fitz barked twice from the back seat. Then he stuck his head back out the window, letting slobber drip off his tongue into the wind. In case you aren't sure, Fitz is in fact a dog.

"See?! Even Fitz agrees," Will moaned, reaching back to pet his friend. "I mean, couldn't we have waited until *after* Halloween?"

"Will, you know we couldn't..." Mom's voice trailed off.

"Yeah, right! Marcellus has only been my *best* friend since first grade, and he's only throwing the *biggest* Fright Fest party ever, and we only coordinated our costumes to be *better* than everyone else's, and now for Halloween I'll probably be sitting at home alone giving candy out to strangers."

This is what Will said. But what really worried Will was Marcellus finding a new best friend. He hated the idea of Marcellus forgetting about Will and the long history they shared. The very idea made Will want to scream. And he was about to. But before he could, he was distracted by a strange man on the street whose whole body and face were covered in bandages and a trench coat. "Look at that poor guy," Will said. "Do you think he's sick? What if this whole town has some kind of weird disease?"

"It doesn't," Mom said.

"Better safe than sorry though. We should probably turn around and go back to New York. Like, now."

"Will, you haven't even given East Emerson a chance!"

"Yeah, well, you didn't give Dad a chance either!" Will snapped.

Mrs. Hunter—or rather, Ms. Hunter—or rather rather, *Ms. Vásquez*, which was her maiden name, and was now her name again—frowned. She took a deep shaky breath and wiped away a tear running down her cheek. As soon as he saw Mom crying, Will's stomach filled with regret.

In a hard whisper, she said, "Guillermo Benjamin Hunter, you may not like it, but East Emerson is our new home—a fresh start, un nuevo comienzo. We need to make the most of it, and that means thinking positive thoughts and treating each other with kindness. ¿Comprendes?"

"Yes," Will answered—though he wasn't sure if he meant it.

Beloved Reader, please, bear with me. Our young gentleman, Will Hunter, will whine and complain and be frustrated with his mother for some time. Personally, I think he is behaving like an immature (and dare I say hormonal) teenager. As someone whose parents dropped him off at the edge of a dark wood and vanished forever after, I find it more than decent of Ms. Vásquez to keep (and even love!) her son in spite of his dramatic behavior…but never mind my opinions. I'm here to tell you Will's story.

I bet this town doesn't even have a comic book store, Will thought to himself. *Now where am I going to get the latest* MonsterWorld *comic?*

He craned his neck out the window. The air felt salty, and wet. They passed a strip mall with all of its stores closed or boarded up. That's when Will noticed a rickety robot clanking down the street. It stopped to speak to a woman, who seemed to be dead—or in this case, *un*-dead. She had on a floral dress and a straw hat with a band of flowers. She was also covered in dirt as though she'd just crawled out of her own grave. As she waved to the robot, her arm fell off at the elbow.

Will rubbed his eyes, then looked again. But too late. The strangers had fallen out of sight, as the car turned onto Ophidian Drive.

On the next block, Will saw an old house with ghosts flying around—and through—its attic. The porch was full of green goblin children stabbing pumpkins with sharp knives. Next door, a haggard old man with a chainsaw dragged a bound unicorn into his garage. A terrible screech ripped through the air. Will craned his neck to look up. Two pterodactyls flew by overhead.

Will didn't believe his own eyes. "What the heck?!"

Then he realized—it was October. Now everything strange made sense. "People in East Emerson must take Halloween really seriously," he noted to his mom. "They're already wearing costumes and doing up their houses and they seem to spend a lot of money on decorations and stuff."

"Really? I hadn't noticed," Mom said. She checked and double-checked the numbers on the street. Finally, she pulled into a driveway in front of a quaint two-story house. "But look—here we are. Our new home!"

Ms. Vásquez stepped out of the car and walked around to the passenger side. She opened Will's door. "Are you coming?"

Will shook his head no.

Mom rolled her eyes. "I'll stand here all night, holding this door open, if that's what you want."

"What I want is to go home," Will murmured.

"This *is* our home now," his mom whispered. "Will, por favor."

Something in his mom's eyes crushed his willpower. He moaned, but crawled out of the car. "Come on, Fitz."

The dog—now Will's only friend in the whole state—leaped out. The Saint Bernard leaned into a long stretch, then gave his massive body a good furry shake. He spotted a garden gnome in the yard, covered in weeds. He rushed over, sniffed it gently, then raised his leg—until the stone statue smiled sinisterly, displaying hundreds of dagger-sharp teeth. Fitz hopped back, raced behind Will's leg, and whined.

Yet it wasn't the gnome that turned Will's stomach. His new yard was pocked with holes and patches of dirt. The mailbox hung sideways like a dying bird on its perch. And the house itself? The windows looked like dead eyes, the chimney stones like bleached skulls, and the walls peeled like a bad sunburn. Worse, the paint was the color of peas. Will hated peas.

"Isn't it just perfect?!" Ms. Vásquez asked. "Once we get some fresh paint on it, it'll be as good as new."

Will tried to say something nice. It came out like this: "I guess it's not a complete dump."

At that very moment, one of the rain gutters fell off with a clang.

"We'll fix that," Mom said.

As soon as Ms. Vásquez stepped inside, she gasped. "Look how big it is! We'll live like royalty here. It's ten times the size of our tiny apartment in Brooklyn. And we have a yard!"

Will surveyed the giant, dusty, musty living room that opened into a dining room off to the side of a large kitchen. The ceilings were white and covered in cobwebs, and more than a few spiders. The floors were covered in an inch of dust and hairballs, and more than a few ants. Worse? The walls were painted the same yellow as pee.

"I liked our old place better," Will whispered. Their apartment had been small, but it had been home. In Brooklyn, he knew where his friends lived, he knew how to get to school, he even knew all the cats at all the bodegas. Here, he didn't know anything. Everything was new—and not in a good way. "It smells like a giant fart in here."

"¡Guillermo!" Ms. Vásquez said. (In all fairness, Darling Reader, it *did* indeed smell like a giant fart.) "I didn't want to move either, but your father—" Mom fought hard not to cry again. "Will, I know that change is hard. But moving is something we had to do. My new nursing job appeared out of nowhere, and the house Realtor practically had to do magic to get this for us. It'll be good. It's our—"

"—our fresh start," Will finished. He hated when his mom cried. He could see how much pain she was in too. So he swallowed his own feelings, and hugged her as she sniffled and wiped her eyes. "Sorry, Mom. It doesn't smell like a fart. It smells like one of Abuela's casseroles."

Ms. Vásquez snorted a little. "Mamá's cazuelas smell like a fart." A small smile crept onto her face. "Why don't you and Fitz go upstairs and choose a room? I'll let you boys have first pick. But grab a box from the car first."

Of course, Will grabbed the most important box first—a longbox of his favorite horror comic books. Will slowly climbed the creaky stairs, Fitz clumsily bounding up ahead. After inspecting the others, Will chose the room at the front of the second floor. It had a large window facing the front yard. He put his comics on the floor and opened it to let some of the farty smell out. Across the street, he saw two kids around his own age in front of a beautiful white house.

The first was a short Black boy with glasses reading a large book on the front steps. He had a high and tight haircut, and a white shirt tucked into pressed khakis. Add a bow tie, Will thought, and the boy could be a young professor. The girl was very much the opposite. As she bounced a basketball around the driveway, scoring rim shots from different angles, her straight, fine black hair bounced around wildly as it streamed out from under her ball cap. She wore a baseball T covered in dirt and stains matching those on her frayed denim shorts and tennis shoes.

The girl stopped dribbling the ball. Carefully, she pulled a small firecracker from her pocket, lit it, and threw it near the boy's feet. BRAK-A-KRAK-A-KRAK-POW!!

The boy started screaming at her, chasing her around the yard, as she laughed. The boy eventually gave up, and went inside. The girl noticed Will watching.

Will waved.

The girl stuck out her tongue at Will.

"Friendly," Will muttered to himself.

Creeeeeeak. The bedroom door swung shut on its own. Will jumped. *Must be the wind*, he thought—until noticing a tiny note stabbed to the closet door by a teeny-tiny broadsword the size of a toothpick. The itsy-bitsy-teeny-tiny handwriting read:

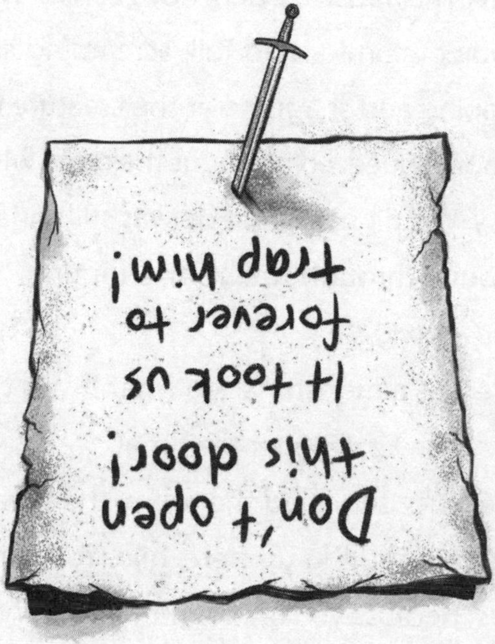

Something banged against the other side of the door. Then again. And again. An icy chill ran up Will's spine. Maybe there was wind in the closet? Or cockroaches? Maybe a stinky cat box, or a dead rat—either the source of the stink? WIll took a deep breath as his fingers wrapped around the knob…

He'd barely turned it when the door burst open and a moth the size of a two-person sofa thrust itself out. It flapped its enormous wings, blowing dust and powder everywhere. The massive insect dove at him. Will tripped over his box of comics and fell, screaming shrilly. Fitz barked, leaping and snapping at the creature to protect Will. The moth squeezed itself out the open window and into the sky. Will didn't realize he was still shrieking until his mom burst through the door, shouting, "*What is it, Will?! What's wrong?!*"

"There was a monster-sized moth!" Will gasped. "It was bigger than Fitz! Bigger than me!"

Ms. Vásquez surveyed the room, then grabbed her chest. "There's nothing up here, hijo. You can't scream like that just because you read something scary. I told you those scary comics are bad for your mind."

"It wasn't the comics, Mom! I'm not imagining things."

"Por favor, Will. We're in an old house, there's bound to be a few creepy crawlers. There's no need to exaggerate about the size."

"I'm not exaggerating!" Will snapped. He went to show her the strange note, but it was gone along with the small sword and the big bug. Will had no proof.

Fitz whimpered. At least Fitz believed Will. Dogs are very loyal that way. Plus, Fitz saw it too. Too bad the Saint

Bernard couldn't explain the situation to Ms. Vásquez. Not yet, anyway.

For the rest of the afternoon, Will quietly carried boxes from the back of the car and helped with the furniture in the moving trailer. Before long, the sun began to set and Will was exhausted. He tried to turn on the TV, but the only channel that worked was black-and-white and the picture was mostly static. The Wi-Fi didn't work either. For dinner, his mom ordered Chinese takeout, but forgot to get the best part—egg rolls.

Mom never forgot to order egg rolls in Brooklyn. And Wi-Fi always worked everywhere. And there was always something to watch—if not on TV, then outside the window on the busy street below their third-floor apartment.

Outside the living room windows, there was nothing. Nothing but quiet houses, creepy shadows, and the chirps of crickets.

"I know it's different, but you'll get used to it," Mom said.

"What if I don't want to get used to it?" Will asked.

Without saying good-night, Will trudged upstairs. He ran the sink water, pretending to brush his teeth. He whistled for Fitz, who jogged upstairs to join Will inside his dark new bedroom. When Will tried to turn on his lamp, the light bulb sparked and went out. "Great," Will mumbled. "I can't even read *MonsterWorld* before bed."

This house was dim and spooky and nothing worked. Will wanted to be anywhere else in the world, but here. But here he was.

Will unrolled his sleeping bag on top of the mattress on the dirty bedroom floor. When he crawled inside, he remembered the first time he used it—camping with Mom and Dad in the Adirondack Mountains in Upstate New York. Dad insisted Will "unplug" for the weekend. No comics, no games, no TV. Will thought he'd be miserable, but he ended up having the best time. Hiking, fishing, swimming in ice-cold streams. His dad made the whole trip worth it—but Dad wasn't here now. How was he supposed to make East Emerson work without the one person who knew Will best?

Will didn't want to, but he couldn't help it—he was wondering about his dad. He wondered if his dad was wondering about him too. A big emptiness opened inside Will's chest—it felt as if he'd lost everything.

It took a long time, but eventually, Will cried himself to sleep.

In Will's dream he was flying. Or floating rather, on a river of cool air. He shivered. When he reached for his sleeping bag cover, it wasn't there. Will blinked himself awake, only to find himself outside—hovering a few feet over the ground. "What the heck?!"

As he shook his head awake, Will fell, his hands and feet sinking several inches into the mud. "Gross!" Will moaned. He pulled at his sinking limbs, climbing onto a nearby stone stair. Raising his head, he found himself on the steps of a mausoleum. He was surrounded by tombstones and holy crosses poking out of the cemetery lots. Will's heart leaped into his throat. He didn't know where he was or how he got here.

An owl hooted above, sitting on the branch of a dead tree with a single word carved into its trunk: JÖRMUNGANDR.

The moon was hidden behind clouds, swallowing the light and making the night darker still. The only illumination came from a bright blue flame flickering at the far end of the graveyard. Will crept past the stone crypt to get a better look, though ducked behind an old tree when he heard the chanting voices.

Thirteen figures, each cloaked in dark robes, stood in a circle around a blue bonfire hovering midair a few feet over a dark chasm. They sang in low voices as a tall woman stepped forward. She pulled back her hood, revealing long purple hair tied into a wild knot that fell into thick and thin braids tied with leather, like some sort of Norse warrior. Will was entranced by the woman's snow-pale face, which was equal parts beautiful and terrifying.

This was too strange. Any minute, Will expected something bad to happen, like in one of his video games that Mom insisted were inappropriate for kids his age. Maybe werewolves would cry out. Maybe the dead would rise from their graves. Maybe a portal to another world or a dark realm would open. Still, Will couldn't seem to make himself leave.

The woman's raspy voice called out in an alien language, her words like broken glass grinding together. As the strange song grew louder, the bonfire flames melted into a brilliant emerald hue. The fire's smoke crackled with electricity, like a mini lightning storm. The woman raised up her tattooed hands and shouted into the growing winds, "Simon! *Eciov ym wollof!*—away from the darkness and into the light. *Uoy ees em tel!*"

The hair on Will's arms stood on end, and his nose filled with the scent of burning ozone. His stomach lurched at the incantation, as though he'd eaten rotting eggs.

In the center of the thirteen, a rift seemed to open. And the crimson ghost of a man appeared, as if made of chalk-colored flame.

"*Em raeh, nomiS...*" the woman whispered in a strange Germanic accent. "I will rescue you. I will bring you back. Do you hear me? I will use my magicks and stop at nothing until you're by my side. No matter what, or *who*, I have to sacrifice to do it..."

Magic? Sacrifice? Will wondered. *Is this woman a...a witch?*

"This you needed to see, to start your true destiny."

The lyrical voice came from a fox, sitting next to Will. She was the color of moonlight, glowing liquid white-silver. Astonished, Will stared at the animal. He whispered, "Did you just...talk? What is all this? What's going on?"

"Oestre's plan starts this eve, to return Simon who

will reave. He'll start by eating a serpent's heart, then destroying the world part by part."

"What? Who's Simon?"

The fox nodded toward the red apparition of the man.

"Simon, can you hear me?" the witch asked.

The ghost faded back into the shadows.

"No! Come back!" In her rage, the witch hit a nearby tombstone. Her fist crushed it into dust and debris. "Bring him back!"

"We can't," said one of the figures, the light of the bonfire reflected in his square-shaped glasses. Two horns peeked out from under the hood of a second figure, his legs that of a goat. "The alignment has passed."

A beam of light balled in the head witch's hand. She threw it at a nearby tree, bursting it into a skeleton of fire.

Will dropped to his knees behind a tombstone, his brow beading with sweat. He pleaded with the fox, "Please tell me what's happening."

"The fates have led you straight to here, to stop the End and conquer fear. You must gather the force of Three, to save this town, then you'll see."

"I don't understand," Will whispered.

"You will," she said gently. *"Find the animals, destroy the crown. Save the animals, and save the town."*

Will lost his balance, and fell backward, onto a dead tree branch. It cracked in half loudly.

"Someone is here, Mistress!" one of the hooded figures called out.

"Search the graveyard!" the witch cried.

The fox turned to Will, her eyes full of fear. Her fur shimmered, then grew brighter, almost hypnotic. *"Return home, to avoid their sweep. Run home, and return to sleep."* Her glow faded as she pushed him with both paws. *"Go now! I will fend them off."*

As if hypnotized, Will's heart calmed and his eyes grew heavy. He didn't understand any of this, yet suddenly, with a long yawn, he didn't care to. The last thing he saw was the fox running toward the witch and her twelve followers. As the fox leaped into the air, she burst into a thousand moonlit sparrow hawks. Lasers and lightning and swirls of magic and flame flashed in the sky as a battle began. But Will, under some spell, didn't stop. He ran straight home, opened his front door, walked up the stairs, and crawled back into the sleeping bag without so much as a second thought.

As the morning sun peeked in through his window, Will blinked awake. He ignored the unpacked boxes littering his room. All he could think about was the strange dream he'd had, with the cemetery and the witches and the glowing fox…

He whispered, "It felt so real…"

But there were no such things as magic or witches or talking foxes. Will laughed until he crawled out of his sleeping bag and saw his hands and feet…

They were covered in mud.

Chapter 2

Strange and Stranger Things

✶

"Will! Will, are you okay?!" Ms. Vásquez screamed. She ran down the hall and burst through Will's bedroom door. She held a baseball bat up, ready to swing at an intruder. Instead, her eyes traced the muddy steps from the stairs to Will's feet.

Dear Reader, as you can probably tell by her screaming, Will's mother was *not* happy. In fact, she was quite scared—that is, until she was furious.

"What! On! Earth?!" she demanded. "Explain, Guillermo. Now!"

Will didn't know what to say.

He stared at Mom. Her hair was a mess, and she still wore her red pajamas. Yet her face was much redder, and her fingers curled into fists that turned her usually olive skin white.

Mom's teeth were gritted together as she spoke. "Five minutes ago, I woke up and thought, *This will be a good day, a good start to our new life in a new town*. Then I walked out of my room and saw three things. One, the front door wide-open. Two, muddy footprints tracked in. And three, said muddy prints leading to your room. Will, I thought someone had broken in! That you might be—"

"Mom, I can explain—" Will started. But he couldn't. His voice faded until he just sat there staring.

Mom collapsed onto the edge of his mattress and sleeping bag. "Will, you can't go walking around a new town in the middle of the night! What were you thinking?"

"Mom, I didn't mean to. I was sleepwalking, except the part when I woke up—but that wasn't my fault. There was this cemetery and these people in cloaks chanting, and a purple-haired woman made the fire turn green 'cause I think she was a witch, and there was a talking fox that—"

"Stop, Will," Mom whispered. She put her head in her hands. "I don't want to hear any stories."

"I'm not making it up!" Will shouted.

"Guillermo Benjamin Hunter," Ms. Vásquez said slowly.

He knew she was angry because she used his full first *and* middle *and* last name. This is what parents do when they are very upset, Cherished Reader, or so I am told. I certainly would not know.

But Ms. Vásquez inhaled and exhaled deeply twice with her eyes closed. "I cannot deal with you acting out right now—"

"I'm not acting out, I'm telling the—"

Mom put her hand up. "I love you, Will. More than anything. More than everything. But right now, I have a new house and a new job and a new town to deal with. I need you to step up and help me out. After school, clean up this mud, and we'll talk about how we can make this transition easier on you. Maybe you can get a job walking dogs, or join a club at school? I don't know. For now, let's forget about this. I need to get you to school. So go feed Fitz, then meet me in the car. Okay?"

"Whatever," Will said. Mom may have been frustrated, but Will was angry. He was telling the truth, and Mom refused to believe him. His dad would have. Dad always believed him, no matter how wild the story. But that didn't matter.

Will's dad wasn't here.

On the drive to school, Ms. Vásquez was quiet. Will (almost) didn't mind. He had too many questions about last night rolling around in his skull. Were the hooded figures really witches? Had he been under some kind of spell? Could glowing foxes really talk? Why did the fox save Will? What had she saved him from? And was all of it real?

It couldn't have been.

The more Will thought about it, the more impossible it seemed. He'd lived in part of New York City his whole life, and he'd seen stuff! People on subways peeing in front of everyone. Thousands of cyclists cycling through the streets naked. Hundreds of Santa Clauses taking over bars around Christmas—okay, well, college kids dressed up as Santa, but still. Will thought he'd seen everything—but nothing like last night.

Still, there had to be an explanation. The first to come to mind was that he *had* been sleepwalking. He'd walked in some mud, but everything else was totally a dream. That was it. It had to be.

Will shook it off. He had bigger things to deal with and he couldn't decide which was worse: Mom being upset at him for something he hadn't meant to do, or starting over at a new school where he didn't know anybody.

On one hand, Mom would eventually forgive him. She might ground him for the rest of sixth grade or until his thirteenth birthday, but she'd still love him. But a new school? He was like fresh meat dangling in front of a lion—that lion being all the other students—ready to rip him apart.

In Brooklyn, Will knew his locker combination by heart. He knew all the city buses to get him to school in sixteen minutes or less. He wasn't the most popular kid, but he had Marcellus. And every Monday, him and Marcellus hosted the Video Game Club after school.

Will already felt lost without his best friend. Add to that, he didn't know where the school bathrooms were located. He didn't know which teachers were nice and which were mean. He didn't know who to sit with at lunch, or if students would be cool or not. And worst of all, this school didn't have a Video Game Club.

It definitely didn't have a Marcellus.

Dear Reader, do you feel awful for Will? I certainly do. Nine times out of ten—children are *not* nice. You see, by nature, human children are cruel. You've probably experienced this yourself. You've probably even been cruel to others yourself a time or two. Do not worry. I am not judging you. After all, I am a monster myself. My point is: starting over at a new school is terrifying. And terror was what Will was feeling right now.

The more he thought about it, the more Will felt uneasy.

"Do I have to start school today?" Will asked. "I could stay home and help you finish unpacking. We could just hang out and and—"

Ms. Vásquez offered a weak smile. "It's better to just get the first day over with, Will. Trust me."

When the car stopped at a red light, Will gazed out the window. In a sewage drain on the side of the street, several people popped their heads up—except they were *not* people. They had little claws instead of fingers. Their faces were furry, having dozens of whiskers on each cheek. They also didn't have eyes.

Will jumped. "Mom! Look! Mole people!"

Ms. Vásquez pinched the bridge of her nose. "Will, there's no such thing as mole people." When the light turned green, Mom drove forward.

"But I saw them!" Will said.

As the car drove near the bay, Will noticed a lighthouse in the distance. In the water below, large fish jumped in and out of the waves. One hopped onto a rock and waved. Only it wasn't a fish. It had an emerald-green tail and blue skin from the waist up. Her teeth were jagged and sharp and she had terrible claws at the end of her webbed fingers. "Mom! A mermaid!"

"Will, stop it. No more stories."

Will began to wonder if his eyes were playing tricks on him. When the car stopped at the school crosswalk, Will looked up. The crossing guard wore a neon vest and had the head of a bull. She also had claws, though they were painted pink.

"Mom! You see that, don't you?! The crossing guard is a minotaur!"

Ms. Vásquez braked the car. She pointed at the crossing guard. "That woman is *not* a minotaur."

"Yes, she is! She has big muscles and hooves and her head is a bull's with giant horns!"

Mom stared at the crossing guard, but shook her head. "Then my eyes must be seeing something else, because all I see is a normal woman. Now, please, stop. I don't want to hear any more lies this morning!"

"I'm not lying!"

"Will, there is no such thing as mole people or mermaids or minotaurs! It's all just…just…*fiction*!"

Esteemed Reader, do recall what I told you earlier: *fiction* means a *not* true story—yet this is a *very* true story. So Will's mom was wrong. But I wouldn't try telling her that. You know how moms can be when they think they're right. Not that I would know about that either…

Ms. Vásquez sighed heavily as she parked her car in front of the school. "Will, I know that changing our lives is hard. But your dad made his choice, and now we have to move on. I promise, in a few weeks, everything will be much easier. Fresh starts take time. Please, *please*, try to have a good day, okay?"

Will felt hot all over. He wasn't making up stories. Was he? Maybe it was true—maybe violent video games and monster comics and scary movies had ruined his mind. No…that wasn't it. Maybe he was still dreaming. He pinched himself. Nope. Definitely awake. Or maybe… maybe this town really was full of strange supernatural things that only he could see—

"Will?"

"Yeah, Mom?"

"You have to get out of the car now."

It took every effort for Will not to slam the door shut. His mom had always believed him before they moved to this dumb weird town. He hated that she didn't believe him now—even if what he was saying did sound far-fetched. Why couldn't she see what he was seeing? Why didn't she hate East Emerson as much as he did? And why wasn't she afraid of new things the way that he was? Will loved his mom, but he didn't understand her—and that made him furious.

Will took a deep breath, ducked his head down, and walked toward the school.

East Emerson Middle was nothing like Will's old school in New York. This building was far larger and older, built with black and gray stones and slats of charred wood, as if the school had survived several fires. Its front red doors looked like a giant mouth, ready to swallow him. The second story had stained glass windows, most of them covered in prison bars—except for those with giant tentacles coming out.

No sooner had Will stepped inside, then a giant furry red devil shouted in his face. "Go, Devils!!"

Will barely stopped himself from screaming. He noted a massive banner in the hallway with a smiling devil in a football helmet on it that read: "Revel the Emerson Devils, 'cause they win on all levels!"

The devil was just a costume. "What kinda school has a *devil* for a mascot?" he whispered to himself. But as he stared back, the mascot winked at him, burst into smoke, and vanished. Maybe it *was* a real devil.

Students swam through the halls like sharks. Some stopped at their lockers, others spoke with their friends. As Will walked down the main hall, he didn't see any signs. He stopped two girls, and said, "Excuse me. Do you know where the office is?"

The girls scrunched their faces like they smelled a rotten egg. The first said, "Ew! He thinks he's popular enough to talk to us!"

"Not even!" the second girl said. They brushed past him.

Will waved at a boy by himself and asked again, "Excuse me. Do you know where the office is?" This boy rolled his eyes and pointed behind Will. "Oh…thanks."

In the school office, the secretary behind the desk found his schedule on the computer and printed it out.

STUDENT CLASS SCHEDULE

LAST NAME	FIRST NAME	MIDDLE	BIRTHDAY
Hunter	Guillermo	Benjamin	*Aug 18*

SEX	RACE	INVISIBLE?	STUDENT ID#
M	Non-Reptilian	NO	*A1-Z26*

PERIOD	CLASS	INSTRUCTOR	ROOM #
1	History	Mr. Rhapaho	*2*
2	English	Mrs. Humphreys	*5*
3	Spanish	Mrs. Hamm	*23*
LUNCH	**LUNCH**	**FOOD**	**CAFETERIA**
4	Math	Mr. Villalobos	*1*
5	Art	Mr. Patel	*18*
6	Science	Mr. Zhang	*5*
7	Gym	Coach Ewflower	*Gym*

PLEASE NOTE: If you see or hear poltergeists, please report to the Principal's office.
PLEASE NOTE: If a werewolf bites you, please report to the Nurse's office immediately.

As Will scanned it, he noticed several odd things. Before he could ask about it, the bell rang. "You better get going," the secretary noted. "You don't want to be late for your first class."

"I don't know where it is though," Will said.

"Linus Cross, would you mind escorting this young man first period?" The secretary waved across the office to a Black boy with deep brown eyes hidden behind thick glasses. Not a single black hair was out of place, and he was impeccably dressed—even if he did look like he worked in an office. The only thing making him look his age was being half a foot shorter than Will, and the red backpack nearly as big as his entire body.

Will gave a little wave. "Hi."

Linus didn't say a word. Instead, he snatched Will's schedule out of his hands and scanned it. "Your first class is in the west hall. I will guide you there. If you have any questions that pertain to our educational institution, I will do my best to answer them. I am also content to not converse at all."

"Oh, well, um…how about we start with *hello*?" Will said. He stuck out his hand. Linus stared at the hand for a full thirty seconds before he finally shook it. Afterward, he quickly pulled out hand sanitizer and cleaned his hands.

"Why do you have such a big backpack?" Will asked. "Aren't there lockers in the hallway?"

"I do not trust my locker," Linus said. "Things always disappear out of it. I suspect my sister stole the combination. She rather enjoys playing pranks on me. Now I carry all of my books and supplies with me along with a few other items in case of emergencies. You can never be too prepared. Now, if you will follow me…"

On the way, Will's head hung low. He'd gone to the same school district his entire life. He'd never been the new kid, and it was an uncomfortable feeling that he wasn't accustomed to. Everyone here was a stranger. Will felt his clothes were all wrong, and he hoped desperately that he wouldn't stand out. But as he trailed after Linus, students seemed to stare. None of them smiled.

"Friendly students, huh?" Will said to Linus.

"Not really," Linus replied matter-of-factly.

"How long have you lived in East Emerson?"

"The entirety of my memory," Linus answered. "It is likely I will remain here through high school, when I will graduate with honors before attending an illustrious university to pursue a doctorate or four in the sciences."

"We're only in sixth grade. Are you really already thinking about college?" Will asked.

"It is never too early to plan for the future," Linus noted, "especially since I'd like to attend either MIT, Harvard, or Stanford. That is why, when I tested well and was presented with the opportunity, I chose to skip a grade. Of course, that complicated my situation upon realizing that it meant I would be the shortest and youngest student in my class, not to mention I would share teachers with my sister..."

"Hey, do you mind if I ask you a weird question?" Will asked.

"I luxuriate in resolving inquiries," Linus said. He pushed the glasses up his nose. "*Luxuriate* means taking self-indulgent delight in something. If I do not know the answer to your query, I am happy to research and find one."

"Oh. Um, okay. It's not that kind of question," Will started. "At least I don't think it is. I was just wondering if there was anything...uh, well, *odd* about this town? I mean, if you've lived here your whole life...have you ever seen anything...unusual?"

"Unusual?" Linus said, scratching his head. "Not to my knowledge. As towns go, I believe East Emerson is quite average and rather conventional."

"Oh. Cool. Thanks." Will couldn't hide his disappointment.

"If there are no further inquiries—" Linus pulled out a book and began to read. With the book in front of his face, Will recognized him.

"Hey! Do you live across the street from me? I moved into the pea-green house on Ophidian Drive. I think I saw you yesterday. You were reading a book, and this girl with a basketball scared you with a firecracker."

Linus pinched his nose in frustration. "It seems we are indeed neighbors. The female to whom you refer is my sister."

"She is? But you two don't—"

"Look alike? No. She is Korean American, and I am Black. We are both adopted."

"That's cool," Will said. Linus frowned. Will realized his mistake. "Oh. No! Not that it's cool that your birth parents gave you up, I mean, it's cool that you have parents who chose to be your parents because they want you, not because they have to, you know, raise you. Um…that came out all wrong."

"I agree," Linus said, "that did come out wrong."

"It's cool that you have a sister. I'm an only child, and it sucks. I have a dog named Fitz, he's kind of like my brother, but you know, really furry. Do you like your sister? She seems…nice?"

"Her name is Ivy, and she is both rude and mischievous. She takes great pleasure in lying, playing with illegal fireworks, and torturing me every chance she gets.

But you can judge her for yourself. I am sorry to inform you that she is in your first class."

Linus pointed to the nearest classroom door. "I highly recommend *not* sitting near her. She is *not* a good student and she will most likely try to cheat off you. Here is your class schedule, as well as a map of the school from the office. I originally drafted this chart for myself, but it seems everyone is often lost within these halls—myself included. If I were not a man of science, I might believe the hallways…change. But that is clearly nonsense. Regardless, you will no longer require my assistance. Have a nice day."

With that, Linus and his giant backpack disappeared into the crowded hallway of students.

Will felt suddenly alone again. Linus wasn't exactly what Will would call friendly, but at least he didn't seem dangerous or mean. Too bad Will had to go and mess it up by making the comment about being adopted. Will smacked his own forehead. "Good one, dummy."

Inside the class, all of the seats were taken except for one—the desk directly in front of Ivy. Ivy was a half-foot taller than Will. She wore torn jeans, a long-sleeve vintage sports T-shirt, and a baseball cap over her straight black hair. She sat back, her feet up on the seat in front of her, drawing on her desk with a thick black Sharpie.

Will decided to ignore Linus's advice. Any connection was better than none. "Hey," Will said to Ivy. "I'm your new neighbor, across the street."

Ivy shrugged. "So?"

"Could I sit here?" he asked, motioning to where her feet were.

"No."

"But all the other seats are taken," Will pointed out.

"Not my problem," Ivy said. "This is where my legs go so I can nap during class."

"Your teacher lets you take naps in class?"

"I wouldn't say he lets me. But he's always so *wrapped up* in the lesson that he barely seems to notice." Ivy snickered at her own inside joke. Will didn't get it.

With no place to sit, he walked to the front of the classroom and waited awkwardly. Will would ask where to sit when the teacher arrived. As he stood there, the entire classroom was staring at him. He forced a crooked smile as sweat beaded on his forehead. His armpits and hands dampened. Will wanted to run back to Brooklyn and Marcellus.

He took a deep breath, and tried not to stare at the floor. With a glance, he realized the students weren't staring at him after all. They weren't staring at anything. Most of them were nodding off, as if exhausted, dark rings under their eyes. The sole exception was Ivy, who looked well rested—probably because she took naps during class.

Will wasn't sure what to think of this school so far.

Dear Reader, if Will had only had the foresight to ask *me*, I could have warned him. But he didn't ask me, and so I didn't warn him. Though I did warn *you* when I told you *not* to read this book. Then again, I suppose if a monstrous creature with my heinous and hideous face tried to dole out advice to me, I would ignore him as you ignored me. So in this case, you were correct *not* to take my advice. What do I know? I'm just a monster…

The first period teacher finally shuffled into the room. He tossed his brown leather briefcase onto his desk and said, "Settle down, settle down. Time to learn some history." But Will couldn't focus. His teacher was dressed head to toe in white wrappings covered in bits of sand and dust. He had yellow eyes and withered brown skin that looked more leathery than his briefcase. The teacher was a mummy.

Will shook his head. Maybe the teacher was dressed up for Halloween. Or maybe he was one of those teachers who wore costumes as different figures from world history, to get students excited about learning. After all, this was a history class.

"You must be our newest student," the teacher said. "I am Mr. Rhapaho." As he leaned in to shake Will's hand, a bandage slipped from his face. What was beneath was—well, just awful. And bloodcurdling. I'd rather not describe it to you, Dreaded Reader, or you'll wet your pants.

Will's scream sounded something like, *"AGGHHHH!"* He scrambled backward to escape, but instead, slipped and fell onto the floor.

A few of the students laughed, but most continued sleeping. Only Ivy sat up and took any real notice.

"You...you're...a muh...muh-muh...*mummy*!" Will stuttered.

"I am *not* your mommy," Mr. Rhapaho said, pulling a pair of glasses from his briefcase and putting them on. "I am your history teacher. Please, take the last open desk in front of Ivy Cross."

Will raced back to the seat in front of Ivy. He shoved her feet off the chair and sat down. Will was breathing so hard and so fast, he got light-headed. His whole body shook. He couldn't help it. He was scared and confused, and to make it worse, none of the other students seemed to notice that their teacher was a real-life mummy. Why couldn't they see what he saw? What was wrong with everyone? Or was it just Will?

That was the moment, Dear Reader, when Ivy leaned forward and whispered into Will's ear. "So you can see the monsters too, huh? And here I thought I was the only one."

Chapter 3

the girl, the squirrel, and the dragon

✶

The bell rang. Class was over. Ivy sped out of the class-room before he could ask her anything—but not before she slipped Will a note. He unfolded the piece of paper and read it:

Nice to meet.
You'll like me.
off and on.
Just remember, the
birds on roof
will poop after
they eat lunch.

“Could everyone get any weirder?” Will mumbled to himself. He crumpled up the strange note and shoved it in his pocket.

His next two classes were English and Spanish. In both classes, most of the students were half-asleep again. He'd half expected kids to either be nice or mean to him today, but no one seemed to care that Will was a new student. Will didn't know whether to feel hurt or relieved. He found he was a little of both. Any attention—even snickers or spitballs to the head—would have been better than nothing.

At lunch, Will didn't know where to sit. He found a table by himself, and ate the bologna-and-cheese sandwich Mom had made. All around the cafeteria, he noticed the other students. Some were laughing or doing homework or eating. Others were yawning, nodding off, or lying on the table asleep.

He missed Marcellus and his other friends. He missed his old cafeteria with its smell of burned Tater Tots and the graffiti murals on the walls. He missed the sounds of sirens outside, and the radio music played on Mondays. He even missed the eighth graders who used to shove him into the lockers. Anything was better than feeling invisible.

When the bell rang, Will got up to wash his hands and walk to class. But as he came out of the bathroom, Ivy grabbed Will, yanked him down a corridor, and dragged him through a red door marked **NO STUDENTS ALLOWED**. She pulled him up the stairs and onto the roof of the school.

"Didn't you get my message?"

"Your weird poem?" Will asked. "Um, I don't really like poetry, and I'm too young to date, so—"

"It was in *code*," Ivy growled, annoyed. "Every third word spelled out a message."

"Huh?" Will said.

"My bad. I thought you being dressed so boring meant you were smart," Ivy said. "Anyway. Let's real talk. How do you see them?"

"You mean the—" Will looked around, then lowered his voice "—the monsters?"

"No, I'm talking about the giant chickens that I just made up," Ivy said. "Duh. Yes, I'm talking about the monsters."

"So you can see them too?!" Will shouted. He didn't mean to, but he was overwhelmed and he couldn't hold it back any longer. "I don't know! I moved here yesterday! At first, I thought your town just really loved Halloween, but today, I saw mermaids and mole people and a minotaur—"

"What's a minotaur?" Ivy asked.

"From Greek mythology. It's a person with the head of a bull."

"How do you know that?"

"I read a lot of monster comic books."

"Nerd," Ivy snorted. "What a nerd."

"Hey! Comics are cool. My dad used to buy me every issue of *MonsterWorld* when it came out and—"

Ivy put up her hand. "I don't care. Let's talk monsters. So Mrs. Mourtain is a mino-toe. Good to know. Don't mind her though, she's harmless."

"Mino*taur*," Will corrected. "And how can she be harmless if she's a monster?"

"Our history teacher is a mummy, the mayor is a sasquatch, and I'm pretty sure the pizza delivery guy is possessed by a demon obsessed with pepperoni. Welcome to East Emerson." With a shrug, Ivy took a piece of gum out of her pocket and popped it into her mouth.

"Why aren't you freaked out about this?"

"I've had time to get used to it," Ivy said. "When I first

got here, I thought I was losing my marbles. Eventually I realized I could see stuff no one else can."

Will asked, "It doesn't bother you, living in a town full of monsters?"

"They're not *all* monsters—" Ivy started. She blew a bubble, popped it, and sucked the gum back into her mouth. She began chewing again.

Respectful Reader, I hope you do not chew gum. It is a filthy, disgusting habit and makes one look like a cow chewing cud. Do you know what *cud* is? Partly digested food returned (as in, *vomited*) from the first stomach to the mouth for more chewing. This happens in *ruminants*, which are animals such as buffalo, camels, cattle, deer, elk, giraffes, goats, and sheep, all of which have *four* stomachs. Four! Who needs four stomachs?! And to think, my parents abandoned *me* for being an abomination. I don't vomit up my food to re-chew it later! That's why no one says life is fair. Because it certainly is not. Now, where was I? Oh, yes...

"—some are creatures from ancient mythology," Ivy continued. "Some are creations of mad science. And others are like, magic things. You know, like urban legends and fairy-tale-type stuff. At least, I think. I'm not much of a reader. I prefer fantasy movies."

"Oh, so reading comic books is nerdy, but watching fantasy movies is okay?" Will asked.

"They're totally different," Ivy said. "My point being, East Emerson's not-normal stuff is all pretty normal here."

"Normal?! There's nothing normal about it!!" Will exploded. He felt like pulling out his own hair. "This town is full of…of…"

I suspect, Silly Reader, the word Will was trying to recall was not *shenanigans*, which is unfortunate, because *shenanigans* is a fantastic (and underutilized) word. Instead, he was trying to think of words that suggested danger, mystery, and terror. Instead he said…

"… INSANITY!"

"Life only upsets you if you let it upset you," Ivy said. She shrugged again, then walked toward the exit.

"That's it? You're going to walk away after you tell me we live in a town full of…of…"

I suspect this time, Dear Reader, the word Will was trying to recall was not *tomfoolery*, which is unfortunate, because *tomfoolery* is another fantastic (and also underutilized) word. Instead he was trying to think of word pairings such as *wretched devils*, or *deviled wretches*. Instead, he said…

"… SUPERNATURAL FREAKSHOWS!"

(Which, Dear Reader, *I* find rather offensive. Remind me to talk to Will about his word choices.)

"Yup," Ivy said. "But I wouldn't recommend calling them that to their faces."

"Wait!" Will called out. "Is there anyone else who can see it? Like the cops, or…or your parents? What about your brother?"

Ivy laughed. "Linus? Not even. Like I said, no one sees this stuff except *me*. And I only see things 'cause of this." She waved her middle finger, showing off a golden ring made up of a golden serpent with a red gem in its mouth.

"That ring lets you see all the weird stuff?" Will asked.

"Yup. If I take it off, weird stuff stops looking weird. Mummies look like normal people, three-headed dogs look like one-headed dogs, and pterodactyls look like clouds. But when I wear the ring, I can see all the secret stuff this town is hiding. I'm the only one. Well, and I guess you now."

"How does it work?" Will asked.

Ivy shrugged. "I dunno."

"Where'd you get it?"

"None of your business."

"Can I see it?"

"No way, dude. No offense, but I don't even know you."

"*You* dragged me up here!"

"'Cause I want to know how *you* see them," Ivy said. "You have a magic ring too?"

Will held up his fingers. "Do you see any rings on my fingers?"

"Chill, dude. No need to freak out."

"Are you kidding?! We're surrounded by…by…"

This time, Ivy finished Will's sentence. "…monsters, myths, magic, and mad science. Pretty cool, huh? Makes this boring little town a lot more interesting."

"It's *not*—" Will started to shout. But by the time he said "—cool," he wasn't sure what he was feeling.

After all, he had grown up reading monster comics with his dad and playing video games with Marcellus and geeking out over fantasy board games with his friends. He'd always loved that stuff because his real life always felt so dull and boring and normal.

But now? Now he was surrounded by all the things

he loved to read about and play games against. However, it was *not* fun. It was…terrifying.

"This can't be real. It can't be. If it is, that means…" Will whispered "…if a monster eats me, I'm D-E-A-D. For real. I don't get a bonus life. I can't start the level over. I can't turn the game off. Oh, god. I have to get out of this town. I have to tell my mom—"

"*No no no!* Don't do that!" Ivy said. "Take my advice. Don't bring this up to anyone. Not your friends, not your parents, and definitely not the cops."

"Why not?"

Ivy hesitated. For the first time, her confidence faded away as she looked at the ground. "When I first realized there were monsters, I tried to tell people…you know, to warn folks. 'Cause here's the thing—even if they saw a giant step on their dog, or a hobgoblin destroy their garden, a second later? They'd just forget about it. Like it never happened. Like there was some kind of magic spell keeping them from remembering.

"They couldn't recall the monsters—but they *could* recall me talking about the monsters. I got into a lot of trouble. No one believed me. Not even my new parents.

They made me go to a therapist. Do you know what it's like when the people you love most don't believe you?"

Will whispered, "Actually... I do."

"Good. Then you know you have to lie. Eventually, I stopped telling the truth too. Said I made the whole thing up for attention. Everyone seemed relieved. Trust me—sometimes it's better to keep the truth to yourself."

"I don't believe that," Will said. "There's got to be a better way."

"There isn't," Ivy snapped. "Or I would have thought of it."

"You could stop wearing that ring."

Ivy touched her ring, staring at it. "That's not an option."

The class bell rang.

"Great. I'm late for class." Ivy picked up her backpack and walked toward the exit.

"Any other advice?" Will asked.

"Actually, yeah. Pretend like you don't see the monsters for what they really are, even when they're staring you in the face with bloodred eyes, razor-sharp teeth, and cannibal breath. They don't know we can see them, and I'd like to keep it that way. So, don't bother the monsters, and they won't bother you. Trust me. You don't want it the other way."

Then Ivy turned around and walked back down the stairs. Will was left alone on the roof, his heart pounding in his chest, as if it wanted to escape.

That night, Will was scared to go to sleep in case he had any more "sleepwalking" accidents. Waking up in a cemetery once was enough. After hours of tossing and turning, he got up, found a rope, and tied himself to his desk. To be extra safe, he also used the dog leash to attach his waist to Fitz's collar. If he went anywhere, his Saint Bernard would hopefully start barking and wake him up.

The next morning, Will woke in his own bed. He'd never been so happy to have clean feet. Not a drop of mud on them. But as he brushed his teeth and took a shower, his dreams weighed on him. The first was about a Brooklyn ice cream truck that insisted on only serving hot dogs. The second was about running into his dad in a restaurant and Dad not knowing who he was, which was awful. And the third was about showing up at school totally naked except for red sequin slippers. Everybody pointed and laughed.

Will felt anxious, but he'd take naked nightmares over angry witches any day.

The second day of school proved stranger than the first. Will saw leprechauns in the lunchroom, goblins in the gym, and bearded banshees in the bathroom. It was hard to...you know, *go*, with an angry death spirit shrieking at him. Will ended up holding his bladder for half the day.

If that wasn't enough, he made a total fool of himself in Spanish class. Mrs. Hamm asked the class, "Clase, ¿Cuál es nuestro capitolio estatal?"

Will answered, "Albany!"

The other students (at least those who were awake) laughed at him. A giant football player named Digby Bronson snorted, and said, "You don't live in New York anymore, new kid."

"Oh. Sorry," Will squeaked.

"Yeah, you are sorry," Digby said. Adding in a whisper, "Loser."

"En español, Señor Digby," Mrs. Hamm said.

"Um...la chica nueva es...una perdedora."

Mrs. Hamm shook her head. "No, Señor Guillermo es no femenina. Es masculino."

"Nuh-uh," Digby said. "Señora Will es muy femenina."

Will felt his whole face flush red. Everyone laughed. Even some of the sleeping kids woke up and got in a chuckle. Digby didn't even get in trouble. Mrs. Hamm just kept teaching. Maybe bullies were considered some form of monster in East Emerson, and Mrs. Hamm forgot.

Dear Reader, this was not the case. Mrs. Hamm was simply trying to be a fun teacher and thought Will was in on the joke. Which he was not. He was homesick for a home that no longer existed. If you have ever been a "new kid" then you know what I'm talking about. If you haven't, consider yourself lucky. Being a new student at a human school is almost as bad as being hunted down by an angry mob with pitchforks and torches. Trust me on this one.

After school, Will walked home alone. He tried not to focus on school or missing Brooklyn or the fact that his dad hadn't returned his last two phone calls. Usually, he would have dwelled and obsessed. But instead, he became quite distracted on his way as he saw a headless horseman, a heckling hobgoblin riding a hyena, a horrible hihi, two heinous hydra hopping on a hopscotch, a hellhound hypnotizing a hippogriff, and two haunted houses. Oh, and a hieracosphinx guarding the hardware store. The least (or maybe *most*) heinous thing Will saw was a hag having honey and tea with a harpy and a heinzelmännchen—which if you don't know, Knowing Reader, is a German household gnome.

Ivy had cautioned Will to leave the monsters alone so they would leave him alone. But it didn't make any of the bizarre creatures any less terrifying. Rather than walking through a new town, Will felt like he was walking through a nightmare. Before long, he was running as fast as he could, ready to get home and lock his doors forever. Too busy looking over his shoulders, Will wasn't watching when he turned the corner—which is how he slammed into Linus.

Will, Linus, and Linus's giant backpack crashed to the ground. Instantly, Linus leaped up, closed his eyes, and swung his fists in the air, shouting, "I will exchange blows with you, good sir! I will engage in fisticuffs upon your insistence!"

Linus swung at the air violently without hitting anything. Will interrupted, saying, “Linus, it’s just me, your neighbor, Will, the new kid.”

Linus opened his eyes. He gazed down at his fists, then released them. He nudged his glasses up his nose, saying, “Oh. Pardon me.”

“What are fisticuffs?” Will asked.

“Fighting with one’s fists.”

“Right. Well, I think you have to keep your eyes open when you fight,” Will said. “That way you might actually connect with something.”

“Naturally. I am still a novice at physical battle, but I am working on an effective defense strategy. I apologize for my overreaction. Some students enjoy harassing me. Thus, my father is trying to educate me on sticking up for myself. It does *not* seem to be working. May I ask, is there a reason you plowed into me?”

“Sorry about that,” Will said.

“Were bullies chasing you?”

“Not yet,” Will said. “I just, uh… I just really wanted to get home.”

“Understandable. The middle school social dynamic leaves a great deal to be desired in an academic setting. I often feel far more intelligent and *perspicacious*—meaning, *insightful*—than my peers, teachers, and most adults. This, along with my brilliance and physical size, often leads to frequent difficult days. People often fear what they do not understand. And people do not understand me."

With that, Linus turned and started to walk away. Will chased after Linus. "Want to, uh, walk home together?"

"Why?"

"Um…because it's the neighborly thing to do?" Will didn't know how to say out loud that he didn't want to walk home alone. "Plus, I really wanted to apologize about yesterday—about the adoption comment. I wasn't trying to be rude or anything. I'm just really nervous, and when I get nervous, I say dumb stuff."

Linus squinted, then raised an eyebrow, as if trying to see through Will. "You seem genuine. Apology accepted."

"Awesome," Will said, "Really. Thanks. For not being, like, a jerk."

"I am many things. A contemptuously obnoxious person is not one of them."

"Right. Cool. So, uh…what do you do for fun around here?"

"I read."

"Yeah? I like reading too. Well, mostly comics and game guides. Do you like video games?"

"No."

"How about comics? My dad bought me a ton of old *MonsterWorld* in trade paperbacks and—"

"I have never had an interest in the graphic novel format," Linus stated coldly. Will's face fell. When Linus saw that, he reconsidered. "Though I suppose you could lend me one. I pride myself on an array of diverse readings—and it's the neighborly thing to do."

Will tried to hide his smile. Something about Linus reminded him of Marcellus.

A bushy-tailed creature leaped down from a tree onto Will's head. Will screamed until he realized it was only a squirrel. It jumped off his head and onto the nearby fence, before scrambling down to the sidewalk.

Linus asked, "Do you have a preternatural fear of Sciuridae?"

"Huh?"

"Sciuridae, the animal family that contains small- and medium-sized rodents, such as squirrels."

"No, not usually. Guess I'm a little jumpy."

The squirrel stood on its hind legs and wagged its

bushy tail. It raised its left arm and waved. Will was about to comment when a three-headed black dog leaped out of the nearby bushes and snatched the squirrel in its mouth.

Instead of screaming, Will grabbed the dog by its spiked triple-collar and shook it, shouting, "Let go! Bad dog!"

The dog struggled, wiggling to escape, almost free. As the dog was about to bound away, Will grabbed it by its tail. The three-headed dog howled, dropping the squirrel. It turned, gnashing its teeth, ready to attack. Thinking fast, Will took off his backpack and swung it, slamming the book bag into two of the dog's faces. The beast yelped and ran away.

"Did you see that?" Will gasped, his heart racing. "A real life Cerberus!"

"No, I did *not* see a three-headed hound of Hades that guards the Greek underworld," Linus noted. "But I suppose you are speaking in hyperbole, a common vernacular among kids. However, I did see you save a squirrel from a common street mutt."

"No, it was a—" Will stopped. He thought of Ivy's advice. Linus was the closest thing he had to a friend. He didn't want to mess it up. "Yeah. Close call."

"That was quite heroic of you. Well done."

"Anyone would have done the same—" Will started.

But words failed him when he saw the little squirrel. It was in bad shape. It looked the way Will felt—chewed up and spit out. "We have to help it."

Linus squirmed. "Do you know how many germs rodents carry?"

"It's a living thing, and it's hurt. I'm not leaving it." Gently, Will scooped the animal into his lunch box.

"Of course, you are right," Linus said. "Let us go get my father. He will know what to do." Hearing the word *father* made Will flinch. He wanted to go to his dad for help too. But that wasn't an option. He tried not to think of that as he looked down at the helpless creature in his lunch box.

As they turned onto Ophidian Drive, Will saw his mom talking to a man at Linus's mailbox. The tall white man with dark hair wore a flannel button-up and a huge beard. Ms. Vásquez waved, calling out, "Will, it looks like you already met our neighbor, Linus. Come meet his father, Mr. Cross."

"Please, you can both call me Ryan."

Mom's smile vanished when she saw the limp squirrel tail drooping over the side of the lunch box. "What happened?"

"A wild dog attempted to eat it," Linus explained.

"We have to help it!" Will added.

Ms. Vásquez's eyes dropped. "Will...we can't afford any extra expenses right now... I'm sorry."

"Actually, our town veterinarian is some kind of famous animal researcher doctor guy. He does a lot of work pro bono," Mr. Cross said. "I'd be happy to drive the boys over."

"Are you sure?" Ms. Vásquez asked. "We'd hate to trouble you."

"No trouble at all. You go unpack, and I'll have the boys back before dinner." Mr. Cross leaned in with a loud whisper to Will's mom, at the same time winking to the boys, "I think it'll be good for *both* our sons to make a new friend today."

"Mom, what have you been saying?" Will moaned.

Then Linus stated, "Father, friends are unnecessary. A distraction even. I am a scholar. Wisdom is my companion."

Mr. Cross squeezed his son's shoulder. "Tell yourself whatever you need to, my little genius. But everyone needs a friend or two. Come on."

"Will, please behave yourself," Ms. Vásquez called as he climbed into the back seat of Mr. Cross's Jeep. She gave her son a telling glance.

You see, Dear Reader, Ms. Vásquez was still frustrated with Will's earlier behavior, but she was also hopeful that Will would make a new friend and stop making up strange stories about their new town. It did not hurt that Linus was a straight A student. You see, parents prefer their children to be friends with straight A students rather than, say, a well-read monster. When I was a child, I tried to find friends and playmates and companions, but it always ended with me being chased out of town by people throwing rocks at my head…

The Jeep pulled up to a new office building connected to a ranch and an old farmhouse. Behind those were several acres of land, fenced in with horses, cows, pigs, dogs, various birds, and some kind of giant green ogre sweeping piles of animal poop into a truck. A large billboard read:

PAMIVER ANIMAL RESEARCH INSTITUTE
& VETERINARY SERVICES

WE'RE HERE TO CARE FOR CRITTERS, BIG
OR SMALL, IF THEY NEED HELP, PLEASE CALL.

ZN R GIFOB VERO ULI OLERMT ZMRNZOH NLIV GSZM KVLKOV?

Inside, Mr. Cross spoke to the receptionist then quickly disappeared with the squirrel and the animal doctor. Will and Linus took a seat in the waiting area.

Brochures about keeping pets healthy filled the coffee table. Next to the reception window was an assortment of collars, leashes, dog whistles, and canned food. There was even a little machine for making pet tags.

Sitting nearby, a young woman held a small fluffy brown puppy. An old man held a fat black cat. And a rather sweet old lady held a birdcage with a small yellow dragon inside it. When the scaled, winged lizard burped, flames burst out. Several magazines nearby caught fire.

Will grabbed the burning papers, tossed them on the floor, and stamped them out with his feet. "Oh, thank you, sonny," the old lady cooed. "That happens at my house all the time. Must be static electricity in the air."

Will nodded to her birdcage. "Or, it might be your evil little dragon."

The sweet elderly woman turned sour. "How rude! My sweet cockatoo bird is *not* evil, young man."

Linus raised an eyebrow at Will. "You are aware that dragons do *not* exist, aren't you?"

"That's what I thought until I moved to this town," Will muttered to himself.

"Still, very impressive how quick you are to jump into action," Linus noted. "Like a hero in the action films my sister enjoys."

Will blushed. Will wanted to say, "I'm not handsome enough, smart enough, or brave enough to do anything heroic." Instead, he said, "Me? I'm definitely no hero."

Mr. Cross finally returned with a heavy frown. Will felt his stomach drop. If a squirrel couldn't make it in this town, how could he?

Linus took a deep breath. "Did the squirrel perish, Father?"

Mr. Cross's frown flipped. "Nah, I was just fooling you! Dr. Pamiver is some kind of miracle worker! I was sure that squirrel was a goner, but Pamiver gave the little furball an injection and a few seconds later, it was up and ready for nuts."

"I'm glad I could help," said a short man with a wheat-ish complexion and strands of black hair combed over his balding head. Will was relieved to find that the veterinarian was an actual person, and not some ghastly goblin or obnoxious ogre.

“The squirrel’s going to make it?” Will asked.

“Absolutely,” said Dr. Pamiver. “The wounds looked much worse than they were. Animals are a resilient lot. Far stronger than people give them credit for. We’ll keep the squirrel here for the next few days. Once he’s healed up, we’ll release him back into the wild.”

Will felt a rush of joy for the squirrel—followed by a tiny pang of jealousy. He wished something as simple as an injection could fix his life.

“You did a good deed today, boys,” Dr. Pamiver said to Will and Linus. “You saved an animal’s life. You should be proud.”

The vet shook their hands. “Oh, and, Will, is it? Mr. Cross tells me you’re new to town and have a dog of your own. I recommend bringing him in to update his shots, always a good idea when moving to a new area. Feel free to bring him by anytime. We love animals here, and we’ll always take care of them.”

“I’ll tell my mom,” Will said, worried about the money.

Dr. Pamiver must have noticed, because he quickly

added, "Free of charge. Consider it my personal thanks for helping our little tree-climbing friend."

"Really? Thanks!"

Maybe East Emerson isn't so bad, Will thought.

As Mr. Cross opened the door to leave, a woman rushed in. Tears streamed down her face. "Mrs. Weaver? Is everything okay?" Dr. Pamiver asked.

"No, it's not!" Mrs. Weaver cried. "My Scottish fold, Priscilla, is missing. Two days now. And you know she's terrified of being outdoors. Someone must have stolen her."

The veterinarian patted her back gently, as the receptionist grabbed some tissues. "There, there," Dr. Pamiver said. "I'm sure she'll turn up."

Mrs. Weaver continued to cry. "I made a flier, with Priscilla's picture and my contact information. May I please hang it up here?"

"Of course," Dr. Pamiver said. "Let me get you some tape."

"It's such a shame," the receptionist whispered to Mr. Cross. "Animals run away all the time. But lately, it seems like it happens more and more frequently." She nodded toward the front wall.

It was covered corner to corner with dozens of flyers for missing pets. Will whispered to himself, "I get it. If I were an animal in this town, I'd probably run away too."

Then he thought of Fitz, and immediately regretted saying it…if something happened to his dog, Will would be crying a lot harder than Mrs. Weaver.

Chapter 4

the black hole

✷

It was finally Friday—which many humans believe is the best day of the week. If you go to school, Schooled Reader, you probably agree. On Fridays, you clap your hands and cry "Hoo-rah!" and celebrate the following two days without teachers and organized learning. You likely even enjoy weekends with friends and family and fun. For me, Fridays are frightful. I never have any plans. No one invites monsters anywhere. But don't feel sorry for me. Please go on and "enjoy" this story. (I hope it gives you nightmares.) (No, I don't. That was mean. I shouldn't have said that. I apologize. Just because I *am* a monster doesn't mean I should *behave* like one...) As I was saying...

It was finally Friday, and Will could hardly believe he

survived his first week in East Emerson. Pixies plagued the post office, a lengthy-necked lizard lorded over the lake, a Winnebago of werewolves warred at a Walmart parking lot, and a famished Fukuiraptor fed on fried food behind a fast-food franchise. Not to mention the Cyclops shopping at the home supply store, a group of robot skateboarders patrolling downtown, and some kind of morose spirit moaning in the mirrors at the movie matinee.

And then there was school…

The librarian was a lamia—meaning she had the top half of a woman, and the bottom half of a serpent. The janitor had a jack-o'-lantern on his neck—meaning his head was that of a pumpkin, carved out to look sinister, and lit from within by a floating flame. And the cafeteria cook was a chupacabra—meaning Miss Maria had green skin, black eyes, gnarled teeth, and spines that ran from the top of her head down to the tip of her tail. She was quite ghastly—though one had to admit she made fantastic food on Taco Tuesdays. Still, Will was continually surprised nothing had made a meal of him yet.

Going to a new school full of monsters was difficult enough. But on top of that, Will found it difficult to make friends. Even the normal human children in East Emerson were a little bit…*off.* Many yawned constantly, nodding off midconversation without even an apology. Most students (and a few teachers) behaved as though they hadn't slept in weeks. Others spent their days looking forlorn (a word that means "pitifully sad"), as though they'd lost something special. For one reason or the other, students moped about school very slowly, like half-asleep zombies.

The good news was that no one picked on Will for being the new kid—an oft-occurring side effect of being the most recent addition to a school.

The bad news was that the other children might be *actual* zombies. Who could tell in this town?

Well, *I* can certainly tell, Dear Reader. These other students were *not* zombies. They were just very, very tired and/or very sad. Why, you ask? Well, if I told you that would give away part of this story, which I am *not* going to do.

As Will opened the front door to his new home, Fitz charged down the stairs, crashed clumsily into the hall table, and tackled Will. The Saint Bernard held Will down with his giant paws, then offered dog kisses. Will couldn't help laughing as the dog's tongue tickled his ears. "Okay, boy, I get it. You missed me. Well I'm home now. And it's Friday, so we have all weekend to hang out."

Fitz barked excitedly, wagging his tail.

The giant dog bounded down the hall and retrieved his leash. He dropped it at Will's feet. Instantly, Will recalled a Christmas, years ago, when Dad brought home Fitz as a puppy. Fitz was this little furry bundle of love. His eyes and paws were so big, but the rest was so small, barely covering Will's lap. Dad smiled, saying, "I know you wanted a game system, but this is way better." He was right.

That Brooklyn holiday seemed like another life. A life where he had friends and a dad and a happy life. Now, he only had Fitz. But not even the massive Saint Bernard could fill the hole in Will's heart.

Will picked up the phone and dialed Dad's number. After two rings, it went to voice mail. "Dad? It's Will. Sorry I keep calling, but I haven't heard from you in a while. Mom and I are in East Emerson, and I—well, I hate it. I wish you were here. Or that I was with you. I miss you, Dad. Call me back, okay?"

Will hung up the phone. His eyes started to burn.

Fitz rubbed his snout against Will's leg, letting him know he wasn't alone. "Thanks, Fitz," Will sniffled. "You ready for that walk?"

Fitz wagged his tail. Will's four-legged friend was the

only creature that made this move bearable. If he didn't have Fitz, he didn't know what he'd do.

Like most dogs, Fitz was an endless source of love for his companion. This is why canines are known as "man's best friend." Admittedly, I would not know. When a dog meets me, it growls, barks loudly, bites me, then pees on my shoes. In that order. Every. Single. Time.

It was a perfect day for a friend-and-dog walk. There was not a cloud in the sky. Which is why Will and Fitz both jumped when they heard:

KRAK-A-BOOM!

Out of nowhere, a storm cloud appeared over the neighborhood. The black billow floated barely thirty feet above the ground, crackling with unnatural neon pink electricity. The cloud couldn't have been bigger than a school bus, and seemed to drift directly toward Will, as if the weather had a mind of its own. Fitz growled.

"You said it, buddy," Will said, scratching his best friend behind the ears. "This town is the weirdest."

Suddenly, Ivy tackled Will and Fitz. She screamed, "Get down!"

KRAK-A-BOOM!!!

The pink lightning attacked the spot where Will had

been standing. It melted the pavement, turning it black. Little wafts of charcoal smoke singed the air.

"You—you—you saved us," Will whispered.

"Whatever," Ivy said. She got up and dusted herself off. Using her foot, she flipped her skateboard into her hand. "You're lucky I was riding by. In East Emerson, you have to pay attention. Next time you see the pink lightning cloud, find cover fast. That thing shoots bolts at people all the time, almost like it's on purpose. No one thinks it's weird—till they're in the hospital. Of course, they immediately forget. Even Mrs. Chang, who has been struck thirty-seven times."

"And she's still alive?!" Will asked.

Ivy shrugged. "Kinda."

Fitz jumped up on Ivy, and licked her face. She scratched behind his massive ears. For the first time, Will saw her smiling. "Hey, good boy! Who are you?"

"That's Fitz," Will noted. "He's saying thanks for saving our lives."

"Awww, anytime, buddy," Ivy cooed. Fitz rolled over so she could rub his belly. "What's with the Band-Aid on puppy's tummy?"

"Mom and I took him to the vet last night. He got a

clean bill of health after Dr. Pamiver updated his shots. Too bad there's no vaccine for lightning. Thanks again. For real."

"It's no big," Ivy said.

"Yeah, it kind of is. I owe you one. A big one." Will picked up Ivy's fallen backpack to hand it to her. "Oof, heavy backpack. You carry as many books as your brother?"

"Nah." Ivy shrugged. She opened her bag to show sports gear. "Linus is the brains. I'm the brawn."

"Can't you be both?" Will asked.

"Nah. Good grades are for Goody Two-shoes. I'm all about the game—football, soccer, baseball, hockey…you name it, I play it. You game?"

"Totally—" Will started, "I mean, like video games. I'm really good at online soccer."

Ivy rolled her eyes. "Not the same thing. No one breaks a sweat playing video games."

"I do. Especially when I play *Mario Kart*."

Ivy perked up. "Oh. Mario Kart's pretty okay. I like to play Bowser."

"Yeah? I play Princess Peach, in the Jeep. You wanna maybe…come over and play—"

Before Will could finish, Fitz took off running. He jerked so hard, his leash yanked itself out of Will's hand. "Fitz! Get back here!" Will ran after his dog. Ivy skateboarded after.

Fitz ran to the end of the street, then turned into a cul-de-sac with three unfinished houses. The Saint Bernard stopped to bark frantically at a gas lamppost. "Fitz, you can't run off like that!" Will gasped, trying to catch his breath as he grabbed the end of Fitz's leash and wrapped it around his hand twice. "Not in this town. Something bad could happen to you."

Fitz kept barking, leaping up and down, trying to climb the lamppost.

"What is it, boy? What are you barking at?"

"Look up," Ivy said.

On the tip-top of the lamppost sat a hare, licking its front paw. It was entirely black except one orange leg, one brown leg, a white ear, and a striped cat's tail—all of which seemed to have been stitched on. Two metal bolts stuck out of its neck, sparking every few seconds. The hare also had a red cybernetic eye and bat-sized, crimson-black dragon wings.

Will rubbed his eyes, as if trying to wake from a dream.

He'd been doing this a lot lately. "Does that *rabbit* have *dragon wings*?"

"It does. And a robot eye. Looks like it went through a blender and got stitched back together wrong," Ivy said. "But actually it's a hare. Hares are bigger, and have longer ears. It's a Franken-hare."

Will whispered, "This town keeps getting weirder and weirder."

Fitz snarled, running in circles at the base of the lamp-post. Franken-Hare didn't seem to notice. It stayed still, licking its mismatched paws.

"I've never seen a Franken-hare before," Ivy admitted.

"I've never seen a Franken-hare before—zzkktt—" something repeated.

"Did that creature repeat what you said?" Will asked.

"Did that creature repeat what you said—zzkktt—" Ivy's backpack repeated. She dug through her sports gear and pulled out a two-way radio.

"This is my brother's walkie-talkie," Ivy said.

"This is my brother's walkie-talkie—zzkktt—"

"Why is it repeating everything we say?" Ivy asked.

"It's not," Will said, eyeing Franken-Hare. The cyborg hare had a little antenna and tiny satellite dish sticking out of the tip of its tale. "The hare is sending out a signal. The walkie-talkie is picking up the radio-wave broadcast."

"It's spying on us?" Ivy asked.

"It's spying on us—zzkktt—"

"Why would a hare want to spy on *us*?" Will asked.

"Faust! Return to base," the walkie-talkie repeated, but this time from a woman's raspy timbre.

"I know that voice," Will said, trying to place it.

"I know that voice—zzkktt—"

"Now, Faust!" the voice commanded. Franken-Hare leaped into the air. But rather than fall, its dragon wings spread out. It flew off into the sky.

"My first night," Will remembered. "I woke up in a cemetery. There was a woman—a witch with purple hair—and twelve others, all hidden in big cloaks. They were doing a spell around a bonfire or something. I thought it was a dream, but the witch's voice, I'd never forget it—and that was her voice on the walkie-talkie. I'm sure of it. I know that sounds wild, but—"

"I believe you," Ivy said.

"You do?" Will asked, surprised.

Ivy smiled. "Dude, this town was built on wild. Where was the cemetery?"

"No clue," Will said. "There was a mausoleum and some trees. One got struck by lightning—"

"I think I know just the one. Come on, let's go check it out."

"You want us to go check out a cemetery where I saw witches?" Will asked. "Doesn't that sound like a bad idea?"

A smirk crept across Ivy's face. "It sure does."

Obviously, Curious Reader, Ivy had not heard the phrase, "Curiosity killed the cat." Or, if she had, she did not heed its warning. You see, my friends, curiosity can be fun, but it can also be dangerous. Being curious leads you to look for things that you should *not* be looking for. Such as Will and Ivy returning to a graveyard, or you reading this book after my warnings. Being curious kills cats. And it might kill you.

Though, to be fair, I must also admit, curiosity may lead you on quite an adventure. And some think adventures fun. Not me. But "some," as in "other people who are not monsters." You see, monsters don't have adventures. They are often the hunted endgame of said adventures. So no, adventures are not for me.

Will followed Ivy through a large field a mile from their neighborhood. As he retold her his memories of that night and that nightmare, they walked. First through tall grass, then over a makeshift bridge of plywood through a marsh area, and finally, past a small forest. "Do you think I dreamed the whole thing, or do you think it really happened?" Will asked.

"I don't know," Ivy said. "But if it is true, and that cryptic fox was trying to warn you of something..."

"Are you as freaked out as I am?"

"I should be, right? But I've lived in East Emerson my whole miserable life, and for some reason I'm used to it. Trust me. In this town, anything is possible."

"Why are you so miserable here?" Will asked.

Ivy held her skateboard over her head as she walked carefully across a log, hopping over a stream filled with flies. "Look at me. I'm Korean, adopted, and love sports in a town that thinks sports are specifically for boys. I don't exactly fit in."

"I'm sure you're not the only one—" Will started. But Ivy cut him off.

"They call me *Monster Girl*."

"Why?"

"Why do you think?" Ivy asked. "Because a few years ago, I wouldn't stop talking about how the town was full of monsters. No one's ever let me forget it. And they never will. Not in a town this small."

Will was going to disagree. But when he stepped over the ridge, he found himself staring at the cemetery from his nightmare. "It's *exactly* how I remember. So that means..."

Goose bumps covered Will's whole body. Hair stood up on the back of his neck. Nausea gripped his stomach when he saw the mausoleum and his own muddy footprints. He found the tombstone shattered by the witch's fist, the tree burnt to a crisp from lightning, and the dead tree carved with the word *JÖRMUNGANDR*.

"...it *wasn't* a dream," Will whispered. "It was all real."

"Cool," Ivy said, excited.

"No! Not cool!" Will said. "That fox was trying to warn me. She said, 'Find the animals, destroy the crown. Save the animals, and save the town.'"

"So?" Ivy asked.

"So if we have to save the town, that means the town is in danger!"

Ivy stepped backward. "What do you mean *we*?"

"It couldn't have been real!" Will argued with himself. "There has to be some other explanation."

He walked away from the graves, toward the plot of land where he'd seen the witches and the bonfire floating over the hole. Ivy followed him. "Where are you going?"

"Why would the fox warn me?" Will whispered. "I just moved here. I don't know anybody. I *am* nobody."

Part of him wanted to run home and tell his mom everything. Except he had already tried that. Maybe he should tell his dad. Would Dad buy him a ticket home? Or at least back to Brooklyn?

But another part of Will wanted it to be true. That part of him moved his feet, one in front of the other. At first he was walking. Then he was running—until Ivy shouted, "Stop!"

He froze on the very edge of a giant hole. He stared down into the pure blackness. But he'd stopped a second too late. His momentum pulled him that one vital inch forward. He teetered toward the gaping chasm…

…until Ivy grabbed the back of his shirt, yanking him backward before he lost his balance.

"Whoa. Looks like I owe you another one," Will admitted, embarrassed.

"If you have twenty bucks, I'll take it," Ivy said. But she

was staring at the large gap in the ground. "What's this hole doing here?"

"It's not a hole, it's a *well*. And someone left a message." Will pointed at the hole's rim, lined with stones, each carved with a letter:

DZGXS BLFI HGVK, 13.
GSV TIVZG WVELFIVI HOVVKH YVOLD GSV OZYBIRMGS,
DSVIV NB SLKV ZMW NB OLEV RH YFIRVW.

Will shook his head. "It's total gibberish."

"Or maybe it's a code," Ivy suggested.

Both Ivy and Will crouched down, staring into the abyss. They couldn't see the bottom.

Ivy pointed at a giant symbol below. "Is that an arrow? Or the letter *V*?"

V

"*Shhh*. Do you hear that?" Will asked. There was a slow and steady *buh-bum, buh-bum, buh-bum*. It took a full minute before Will started, "Is that—? No. It can't be—"

"—a heartbeat," Ivy finished. "But how can a well have a heartbeat?"

Will picked up a pebble and tossed it into the darkness. He and Ivy waited for it to make a sound when it hit the bottom. But it never did.

Chapter 5

The Storm of Shadows

✷

As most humans do, Will needed an alarm clock to wake him each morning. Usually, that alarm clock was Fitz. Fitz was a rather happy dog who enjoyed licking Will's face (and not *biting* it as dogs do to mine). But this Sunday morning, Fitz did *not* wake up Will.

When Will finally opened his eyes, it was because his mom was calling from downstairs. "Lunchtime!"

"Fitz?" Will said. He whistled, but Fitz didn't come. This was unusual. Will walked downstairs with a bad feeling in his gut. "Mom, have you seen Fitz?"

"He's not down here," Ms. Vásquez said. She put groceries away in the cabinets and fridge. "He's not in your room?"

"No."

"Well, he has to be in the house somewhere. It's not like he could have..." Ms. Vásquez's voice trailed off. The back door was open.

"Oh, no," Ms. Vásquez whispered. "I was bringing groceries in from the car and I propped open the back door. I didn't—"

"Mom, what were you thinking?!" Will snapped, panic rising in his throat. "It's a new town. He could be lost. What if he falls down a well, or gets eaten by an evil Easter bunny?!"

Ms. Vásquez fished in her purse for her smartphone. "First of all, he won't be eaten by an Easter bunny, because there's no such thing—"

"That's what *you* think," Will mumbled.

"—and second, this kind of situation is exactly why we had a microchip put in his collar. So we can track him." Mom tapped at her phone, opening the dog tracker app. After a moment she said, "He's right...oh. He's not showing up."

"See?!" Will said. He shoved his feet into his shoes and grabbed his jacket. "I'm going to look for him."

Ms. Vásquez grabbed her own jacket and the car keys. "We'll go together."

Will and his mother drove around for hours looking for Fitz. They drove through the neighborhood three times, then circled around it, going to the park, the school, the town square, even to the lighthouse on the east beach. There was no sign of Fitz. As the day got later, the terrible knot in Will's stomach grew.

"I'm sure he's okay," Ms. Vásquez said. "Dogs are curious animals. He probably just wandered off to get a lay of the land or chase a squirrel."

"This town is dangerous," Will said. "You don't know what's out there."

"What's that supposed to mean?"

Will didn't know how to answer. You see, Mature Reader, adults are lovely people, but they often do not listen to children. Grown-ups believe they know everything. Which, believe you me, they do *not*. By being married to their beliefs, they close their minds to any and all extraordinary possibilities. It is an unfortunate side effect of growing older. I hope you never grow older. I certainly will not, but you do not need to know about that. As I was saying...

Will felt stuck. Ivy had warned him about the truth, but he wanted to tell Mom everything. Ever since their first argument about East Emerson, Will wanted to convince his mom about the impossible things he saw, even if she didn't wanted to hear it. He hadn't pushed because he didn't want to upset her. But now? Fitz might be in danger. He couldn't hold back. The truth came spilling out, like water through a cracked dam.

"Mom, we need to find Fitz and leave East Emerson. There are monsters and magical creatures and mythological beings and mad science experiments just walking around town. And no one can see them—except for me for some reason. And Ivy who says the monsters are harmless, but I don't believe her. This place is cursed. We need to leave, before it's too late."

"Will, that's enough!" his mom shouted. She parked the car, her face burning red. "I am sorry for yelling but *please*, Will, no more made-up stories. No more lies. We are *not* going anywhere. East Emerson is our fresh start. It's a lovely town, and it's our new home."

"No, it's not!" Will argued. "This is *not* our home! Our home is with *Dad*!"

"STOP, WILL! JUST STOP!" His mom's shouts melted

into tears. The silence in the car felt thick, like there was some large chasm between Mom and Will. He wanted to fight, to scream the truth. But his mom made it clear she would not hear it.

When Mom began again, her voice was shaking. "Even if I did believe you—which I *don't*—we can't leave. We don't have any more money. I spent every last nickel and dime I had getting us down here, and putting down a deposit on the house. For the foreseeable future, we'll be living paycheck to paycheck. I barely have enough money for groceries as it is. So we have to make this work. We don't have any other choice."

"But Dad—" Will began.

"Will, *he left us*. He *left*, and he's not coming back," Ms. Vásquez said.

Will didn't want to hear it. He didn't want to believe it. Even if he knew it was true. You see, Honest Reader, sometimes when a person is faced with a difficult truth, it's easier just to ignore it. But the truth is like the sun, one cannot hide from it for long. Eventually, it will come out, and you'll have to face it. Will knew the truth, but he still wasn't ready to accept it.

Ms. Vásquez reached across the car and took Will's

hand in her own. She squeezed it. "I know this isn't what you want, but we need to make East Emerson work. I'm sorry you hate it here, but what's done is done. We're staying. Please, *please*, give it a chance. I know we can make a new life for ourselves, if we just try."

Will had never seen his mom like this. Her eyes had dark rings, like she hadn't slept. And her face looked decades older somehow. She couldn't even meet his gaze. Will realized that she was overwhelmed too. She was angry and sad and even...afraid.

Just like Will.

Will's stomach churned. He felt sick. Not just about Fitz, or being stuck in East Emerson with witches and talking foxes and monsters, but about his mom. He didn't know about the money—or the lack of it. He didn't know Mom was struggling. Though it explained why Mom had gone grocery shopping but there was still nothing in the cabinets except one jar of peanut butter and some dry ramen packets.

Will felt awful for bringing up his dad. But he also felt scared. Not just of the strange things in town, but of going hungry.

"I'm sorry," Will whispered. "I didn't know about the money."

"I didn't want you to. I'm the adult. It's *my* job to take care of things. And I will. But I need you to help me. Can you do that? No more made-up stories about this town, okay? Promise me."

It made Will sad and uncomfortable that his mom was asking him to lie to her. But Will needed to see her smile. So he said, "I promise."

Ms. Vásquez restarted the car. "I'm sure Fitz is fine. I bet he's just out chasing a cat. He's probably waiting at home for us right now."

Usually, moms are right about such things, Dear Reader. Or so I have heard. I certainly wouldn't know from personal experience. But in this instance, Will's mother was wrong. Fitz was *not* waiting at home for them. When Will discovered this, a dark cloud fell over him. Darling Reader, if you've ever had a pet that you loved and loved you in return, you might know what a negative feeling it is to have that best friend suddenly vanish. It's the worst feeling in the entire world. I would not wish it on anyone. Not even that wicked, vile Santa Claus...

"Oh, mijo. I feel awful," Ms. Vásquez said. "I want to

keep looking, but I can't. I have to go to work. It's my first week at the hospital, and I can't miss it."

Will couldn't say anything. He was fighting back a hot burning sensation behind his eyes.

His mom hugged him, squeezing him tight. "Fitz is such a friendly dog. I bet he got picked up by a Good Samaritan. As soon as they see his collar, they'll call my cell phone. I tell you what, I'll leave it here with you so you'll be the first to answer. Okay?"

Will nodded. His mom hugged him again, then kissed his forehead. As his mom left for work, all Will could think about was Fitz. What if he couldn't find his way home? What if he was hurt? What if he'd been devoured by a dinosaur or a demon or a dragon or a diwata or a devilish dybbuk or a dark dryad or a duplicated doppelgänger?

After twenty minutes of staring at his mom's phone, waiting for it to ring, Will decided he couldn't just sit around any longer. He pulled his bike out of the garage, and rode out to look for his dog. He had two hours until the sun went down, but he would search all night if he had to in order to find Fitz.

Will rode up and down the streets, whistling and calling for his friend. He passed a row of restaurants with names including Pizza Pie Till You Die, Death by Tex-Mex, Coffee Monster, Meat Murder B-B-Q, Headless Horseman Pasta House, You Scream for Ice Cream, and BILL'S CHICKEN GRILL—only the letter *G* was gone and part of the *R* had fallen off, so it said BILL'S CHICKEN KILL.

Back in Brooklyn, Fitz liked to sniff restaurant trash, so Will hoped to find Fitz passed out behind one of the dumpsters. No such luck. Though there was a group of goblins fighting a swarm of sprites over old pizza and chicken wing bones, but no sign of a Saint Bernard.

Beep-da-leep!

An alert appeared on his mom's cell phone—it was the dog tracker app. It had a ping on Fitz. Will pulled up the map, then sped off on his bike. He followed Main Street to Ekans Avenue, then along an unpaved dirt road heading south. To the west, giant hills rose up ominously, and to the east was a winding creek. The hills, water, and road met at a huge empty lot laid out before a dilapidated amusement park. As Linus would tell you if he were here, *dilapidated* means "in a state of disrepair, generally caused by neglect or the passing of time." It's another way to say "old" or "falling apart" or "abandoned," like a once-favored toy that you've outgrown. Or like me, by my own parents. Or like your grandparents. (You really should call them more often.)

Beep-da-leep. Beep-da-leep. Beep-da-leep.

According to the phone's chirps, Will's dog was getting closer. "Fitz!" Will called. "Come here, boy!" He used his fingers to whistle as loud as he could. He listened, but heard nothing but the wind.

Will dropped his bike against an old fence, and stared up at a faded sign.

WELCOME TO
SVENGALI FAIRGROUNDS!!
WHERE CHILDREN COME TO ~~PLAY~~!
DISAPPEAR!

Someone had scratched out the word "play" and replaced it with "disappear." But that wasn't what sent shivers up Will's spine. It was another message that had been carved into a nearby pillar. The letters were similar to those at the well in the cemetery:

GIVZW ML UFIGSVI, 13.
GSRH RH XOLDM GVIIRGLIB.

Holding up the marquee were giant clown statues—their paint flaking away, making them look as if their face paint was peeling off to reveal horrible green-scaled skin beneath. Another chill rushed through Will's body.

Will was terrified of clowns.

His hands were shaking, but Will steeled himself. If Fitz was here, he had to find him. The fairground gates were locked, but the old wooden fence was falling down in several places. Carefully, Will climbed over and crept inside.

Decades before, this large outdoor fun-space had been filled with games, rides, refreshments, and other forms of entertainment. Now it was filled with rats, snakes, and long shadows as the sun began to set. All of the once-bright colors had faded into drab, mute shades of gray and sun-beat pastel. The Ferris wheel looked like a giant spiderweb, the roller coaster like a death trap, and the funhouse like a haunted house—though that may have been because the funhouse was also a haunted house.

"Fitz! Here, boy!" Will called out again.

His voice echoed in the nooks and crannies of the deserted park. The entire place was quiet except for the crinkle of trash wind-blown across the broken sidewalks. Despite the eerie silence, Will felt like he wasn't alone. Like he was being watched.

Beep-da-leep. Beep-da-leep. Beep-da-leep.

The phone said Fitz was only thirty feet away. Will raced forward. Twenty feet… Fifteen… Ten… Five… Two feet…

Beep-da-leep. Beep-da-leep. Beep-da-leep. Beep-da-leep. Beep-da-leep. Beep-da-leep.

When Will looked up, he screamed. *"Arghhh!"*

He fell backward and scrambled away before realizing the monstrous clown in front of him was just another statue. It held a bouquet of plastic balloons—though over time, they'd melted into what looked like white skulls on the ends of thin swords.

"I'm here to find Fitz. I'm here to find Fitz," Will repeated to himself. He checked the phone again. Zero feet. Fitz should have been right here.

Will scanned the area again. There was nothing except the terrifying clown, an old popcorn stand, an entrance to a park feature called the Cave of Doom, and… Fitz's collar lying on the ground.

Will picked up the collar. As his fingers grazed Fitz's

name, he recalled the trip to the pet store with Dad, who let Will pick out the collar and the silver tags. Will's heart dropped into his stomach. It felt as though he'd been punched in the gut.

"Fitz!" Will screamed as loud as he could. Then he whispered, trying not to cry, "Where are you, boy?"

As he held the collar in his hand, Will realized that dogs can't take off their own collars. So Fitz wasn't just missing. Someone must have taken him.

The sun began to dip behind the western mountains, turning the sky into a blood-tinted orange. The shadows grew long, distorting themselves into menacing shapes that taunted Will. He wanted to stay and keep looking for Fitz, but some instinct told him to get out of there. Now.

Out of the corner of his eye, something stirred. Will turned. Nothing—except now there were *two* clown statues. Hadn't there been just the one with the skull-like balloons? Now there was a second with a giant mallet. Will gulped. Maybe he just hadn't noticed?

Something flashed in the corner of his other eye. He turned again. A third clown statue stood there, smiling a creepy smile, its face paint peeling away. This one held a pie in two hands, except the cherry pie looked like it was dripping blood. Will shivered. Another movement, then another. Will spun around again, then again. A dozen clown statues surrounded him. Will whispered, "But you can't move. You're just statues, right?"

The clown closest to him slowly shook its head from right to left. Then its smile melted into a frown and its eyebrows dipped inward until it was scowling. Roaches and centipedes came crawling out of its pie.

Will wanted to run away, but he couldn't move.

Fear froze him solid.

Kind Reader, surely you are not judging young Will for being petrified. What is your worst fear? Heights? Germs? Enclosed spaces? Snakes? Butterflies? Whatever it is, I am certain you would be frozen with fear too if you found yourself surrounded by it. What's *my* phobia, you ask? Ha. Good try. I am not telling you. You could use it against me like my archnemesis used to do. No thank you.

Will was surrounded. The clowns approached inch by inch, their hands slowly rising up, ready to grab Will if he tried to run. There was nowhere to go.

RUUUMMMBBLLLEE!

The ground shook and thundered like a subway train was rolling by underneath. Horrible screeching and growling ripped through the air. The sound made Will's skin crawl. But whatever it was, Will was grateful. As soon as the clowns heard the cries, they forgot Will. All of them turned and ran.

Will's relief was immediately replaced by a new fear. If clowns—which were terrifying—were terrified, whatever they were terrified of must be even more terrifying. (That does make sense, does it not? I just reread it. And yes, yes it does.)

Something inside Will told him to run. So he ran.

Behind him, a burst of wind and debris blew out from the nearby Cave of Doom entrance. A second later, a giant swarm of darkness exploded from it—shadows and dark shapes of all sizes swarmed out from the cave mouth, as if vomiting up a storm of flying creatures.

Will leaped the fence and grabbed his bike. He pedaled as hard as he could, turning just in time to see the sky darkened by bats and birds—but there were more creatures alongside them. Hundreds of shapes, maybe thousands. Each was different and unique, yet all of them were flying in a maelstrom of shadows just below the light of the setting sun.

Will wasn't sure what was racing faster: his heart, his thoughts, or his feet on the bike pedals. He sped along the old dirt road toward town. Behind him, the swarm of creatures spun in an intimate circle just above the Svengali Fairgrounds like a massive school of fish. They stayed out of the sunlight, as if afraid of it. Will thought he was safe until the sun dipped lower and the swarm shifted toward the road.

They were coming after Will.

At this moment, Dear Reader, you may be frightened. But I assure you, there is no need to worry for me. I am safe and sound in my humble shack, typing this story for you on a very cranky typewriter. What's that? Oh. You're not frightened for me, you're frightened for Will? Right. Yes. Of course you are. No one cares about an author. I see. Never mind. Continue on…

That's when Will saw sunlight at the end of the road. The shadow of the high western hills ended there. If he could make it to the sunlight, maybe he would be okay. The swarm hadn't come out until the sun had gone down, maybe it—whatever it was—was allergic to sunlight.

Goose bumps and sweat covered Will's body. His heart pounded as he pedaled harder. A stitch stabbed in his side. The swarm was almost on top of him. He tried to look back, but all he could see was a flurry of wings and tails and red eyes of every shape and size. He pedaled harder than he'd ever pedaled before. It felt like his heart might explode or his legs might catch fire, but he kept going.

Something nipped at the back of Will's neck. Was it mosquitoes? Was it whiskers? Was it teeth? He didn't know, and he didn't care. He rode his bike harder and faster than he'd ever done before—which is the exact moment when his tire hit a rock.

Will flew over the handlebars and skid across the dirt road. Will was sure the swarm had him now. He curled up and raised his arms in defense. He didn't realize for several seconds that his eyes were closed and warm sunlight drenched his body. He slowly blinked, then looked. From this spot, the sun still had a few more minutes until it finally set.

When he looked back to see if the flying beasts were waiting for him, he discovered the swarm gone. There was nothing in the sky except perfect pink clouds.

Chapter 6

the secret history

✶

"Please eat something," Ms. Vásquez said.

"I'm not hungry," Will snapped. He shoved his breakfast plate across the table.

"Will, I know you're upset—"

"Upset? Upset doesn't begin to cover it, Mom! I found Fitz's collar in an old amusement park, where I was almost—" Will remembered his promise. His mom didn't want to hear any more *stories*. Except these weren't stories. They were the truth. But she didn't want to hear the truth.

Ms. Vásquez rubbed her temples. "Mijo, I know you're upset about Fitz, but you cannot ride your bike to strange places by yourself. It's dangerous."

"Well, if it's dangerous for me, imagine what it's like for Fitz."

"I'm worried about Fitz too. But *you* are my priority. Since he left—"

"Dad left. Fitz was taken," Will mumbled. "We have to find him."

"It's only been five days since Fitz—" Mom didn't—or couldn't—finish her sentence.

"Five days is forever. What if he—" Will didn't—or couldn't—finish his sentence either.

"We have to stay positive. We have to believe he's okay," Mom whispered. Though Will could hear the strain in her voice.

Will felt like a balloon being overfilled—except instead of water, he was filling with rage. And he couldn't stop himself from bursting. "We should *never* have moved here! I told you something was wrong with this town when we got here but you wouldn't listen!"

As he stormed out of the house, he slammed the door as hard as he could, shouting, *"This is all your fault!"*

Dear Reader, you might think that Will was being dramatic, or behaving like an abominable brat. But try not to judge him too harshly. I suspect you too have behaved this way toward your parent or guardian at one time or another. Sometimes when things get tough, we lash out at the ones closest to us. That is natural. Though it is also rude. After all, sticks and stones may break bones, but words hurt people for years and years after they are said. I've been called many names by my loved ones, and they were far more hurtful than the spears and swords I've been stabbed with.

On the walk to school, Will felt sick. He wasn't sick, mind you, Adored Reader, but he felt sick. Like his stomach was upside down with a large rock in it. He did not have gas or indigestion. No, he was upset. Yes, he was upset with Fitz missing and at having been forced to move farther away from his dad (even if his dad had left first), but he was also upset with himself. He felt bad for shouting at his mom. He shouldn't have been so harsh. Even if part of him meant what he'd said...

He tried to swallow down his guilt, and focus on hope: Fitz had to be alive. He was—*is*—a tough dog, Will thought. The toughest! Maybe someone tried to take him, and nabbed his collar, but didn't get Fitz. Maybe he was still out there, hiding, or lost. Will had to keep looking.

For the last two days, Will had been posting fliers

all over town. He'd taped them to signs, tacked them to poles, hung them at bus stops, and stapled them to community boards. Will even went to the animal clinic, where Dr. Pamiver let him hang one in the lobby. But everywhere he went, he noticed more and more fliers for other people's missing pets. He began to wonder if East Emerson itself was swallowing the animals.

Will's stomach fluttered. It was not filled with butterflies—but with mosquitoes, killer bees, and deadly spiders.

Once he got to school, he walked straight to the copy machines in the library. He'd run out of fliers for Fitz, and he needed to make more. As the machine spit out the last ten copies, Will saw Linus reading at a table. He crossed the room and tapped his neighbor's shoulder.

"*Who goes there?!*" Linus shouted, as he jumped from his chair, knocking over a pile of books.

"Sssilence! Thisss isss a library, not a gymnasssium!" the librarian hissed as she slid across the floor. By *hissed* and *slid*, I do mean *hissed* and *slid*. In case you forgot, Respected Reader, the school librarian was a lamia. Besides their serpentine bodies, lamias are well-known for their ferocious fangs which they use to devour children.

What? Don't be upset with me if that frightens you. *You* are the one who chose to read this book after I warned you against doing so.

"Apologies, Ms. Campe," Linus said.

"Yeah, sorry," Will gulped. He forced himself not to leap back when the lamia glared at him with her purple eyes. He took a deep breath and reminded himself to behave as if all was well. He gave his most charming smile, adding, "Won't happen again."

The librarian lamia adjusted her glasses and nodded back politely. She slid away with a pile of books to reshelf.

It seemed to Will that Ivy's advice held. He didn't bother the lamia, and she didn't bother him. Though probably only because she didn't know that he knew what she knew about knowing what she really was. Right?

Will returned his attention to Linus. "Sorry, I didn't mean to startle you."

"You are not accountable. I forget reality when delving into vast tomes of knowledge," Linus stated. "Books are often my only respite from the reality of a boring, mundane society where intelligence is ranked below physical stamina." Will must have had a blank look on his face, because Linus explained, "I get lost in books easily."

"Cool," Will said. "Um, any chance you've seen my dog around our neighborhood? Or anywhere else? He's missing."

"I have not," Linus said.

"Oh. Okay. Well, any chance you know where to hang fliers here at school?"

"The bulletin board next to the central office," Linus said. "I was about to go there myself in case someone has located my science textbook. It has been absconded from my backpack. I suspect my sister, but she pleads innocence. I will walk with you."

As the pair walked down the hall, Will noticed a student's locker trying to eat her. She squealed and pulled her arm free. A single second later, the same student seemed to forget and reached into her locker again, with similar results.

"Maybe your locker ate your book?" Will suggested.

Linus raised an eyebrow at Will and shook his head. "You sound like my sibling—who is hailed locally as a ridiculous charlatan. I recommend *not* following her path."

"Someone say my name?" Ivy asked, appearing behind them.

"No," Linus said. "Unless you've earned another detention from an educator."

"Sick burn, brother," Ivy said sarcastically. "What's shaking, neighbor? See any more monsters?"

Linus looked at Will who looked back and forth between the brother and sister. He wasn't sure if Ivy was trying to test him to see if he'd say something or not. "Uh... what monsters?"

Ivy winked. "Good answer."

As the trio arrived at the school announcement wall, Will's hope fell. This wall of fliers was twice as big as the vet office's wall, and it had almost three times as many posters asking about lost pets. Each started with the same word: *MISSING*.

Missing dogs. *Missing* cats. *Missing* rabbits. *Missing* hamsters, lizards, snakes. *Missing* mice, birds, ferrets, parrots, turtles, and tarantulas. There were even fliers for a *missing* sugar glider, a *missing* potbellied pig, and a pair of *missing* Madagascar hissing cockroaches named Lisa and Louise Burns.

A girl was adding her own poster to the wall. Tears streamed down her face. Will asked, "Are you okay?"

"No, I'm not," the girl sobbed. "My chickens've gone missing."

"As in your meat lunch or your domesticated fowl?" Linus said.

"My pets! I have a dozen of them. I raised them up from chicks. Every morning, I walk out to collect their eggs, and the girls come a'running. Till this morning. I went out, and they're gone. No sign of foxes or cage tampering or anything. Just...gone. Like they flew away—except chickens can't fly."

"I'm so sorry," Will said. "I hope you find them."

"Yeah, I hope they aren't chicken *nuggets* by now," Ivy said.

The girl burst into more tears and ran down the hall.

"You are ghastly," Linus said to Ivy.

"What? She calls me Monster Girl all the time. Plus, I'm just preparing her for the worst-case scenario," Ivy said. "Well, worst-case for her. Best-case for me. I love chicken nuggets."

Will stared up at the wall of *Missing* fliers. Something pulled at the back of his mind, but he couldn't recall what exactly. "This is bananas."

"I do not see the correlation between yellow fruit and

the parallel irresponsibility of so many children having lost their pets," Linus noted.

"It's a metaphor, dingbat," Ivy said.

"Do you even know what a dingbat is?" Linus asked.

"Stop talking for a minute!" Will snapped at his neighbors. "Look at this. How is it possible that *all* of these kids have lost their pets in such a short amount of time? And it's not just kids. Linus, remember the vet's office? Same thing. Pets all over East Emerson have gone missing. Doesn't that seem like too much of a coincidence?"

"That's because the pets haven't been lost," Ivy said, "they've been *pet-napped*."

"And what evidence brought you to such a far-fetched conclusion?" Linus asked with a roll of his eyes.

"Onenay," Ivy said. *"Ustjay away utgay eelingfay."*

Linus snorted. *"Owhay eryvay ientificscay ethodmay ofway ouyay."*

"Huh?" Will asked. "Are you two speaking Hungarian or something?"

"Awesome, right? It drives our folks nuts," Ivy said with a grin.

"Igpay Atinlay," Linus explained. "Pig Latin."

Will shook his head, trying to focus. "I'm never going

to find my dog, am I? With all these other pets missing, what are the chances I'll find Fitz?"

"Oh, no, for real? Fitz is missing?" Ivy asked. Will was caught off guard by the concern in Ivy's voice. It was the first time he'd seen her express anything besides being smug.

Will nodded. He looked across the board for some free space, but there wasn't any. He decided to just tape his on the empty wall next to the others. His color copy looked so lonesome by itself. Especially with Fitz's picture under the word *MISSING*.

"Why would someone pilfer the local domesticated animals?" Linus asked.

"To see if they could?" Ivy shrugged. "I don't know. Maybe someone cooks them and eats them."

"That is both absurd and awful," Linus observed. "Next you'll be saying that the animals have become the meals of Saci, Sagari, Sasquatches, and cyber sentinels."

"Maybe a local coven of witches needed more familiars," Ivy hissed. "Or an eccentric hypnotist is training them for a new circus, or a centaur is saving them from bad pet-parents, or the government is turning them into a cyber army! Who knows in this town?!"

"Don't even kid around about that stuff," Will whispered, looking in both directions to make sure no one was listening.

"Who's kidding?" Ivy said. "You know what East Emerson really is."

"Ivy, now is not the time for your inappropriate humor," Linus stated. "I am accustomed to your depraved sense of comedy, but our neighbor is dealing with a personal crisis."

Ivy grabbed Linus by the collar. "I've told you a hundred times, Linus—*I'm not kidding*. This town is full of the supernatural."

"I have seen no empirical proof to support your claim."

"Yeah, well, Will can see them too! Tell him, Will!" Ivy snapped.

Linus and Ivy both stared at Will, waiting for an answer.

"Well, uh..." Will stammered. He thought of how his mom looked at him when he told her the truth. He didn't want Linus to think he was a liar too. But he also didn't want to lie. "There are, uh...definitely some...*strange* things going on in this town."

"Strange things? *Strange things?!*" Ivy groaned. "There's a lot *more* than strange things in East Emerson—"

You said not to tell anybody! Will mouthed behind Linus's back.

"Yeah, well, Linus thinks he's such a know-it-all. He deserves to be taken down a peg or two," Ivy growled. Then, in an almost silent whisper, she added, "I don't care what the rest of the town thinks, but he's my brother. He should believe me."

"I apologize profusely for my sister's behavior," Linus interrupted. "Our parents have tried to help her seek counseling."

"Linus, one of these days, you'll find out I was right, and you'll regret ever doubting me about all of it—the ghost pirate ships, the lizard people living underground, the unicorns in the woods, the zombies, Bloody Mina hiding in mirrors—" As Ivy counted the weird happenings on her fingers, her voice grew louder until she was practically shouting. Students and teachers began to stare.

Linus tried to put his hand over Ivy's mouth. "Once she gets started, my sister goes on a twisted tirade of nonsensical nonsense about *monsters* and *myths* and—"

Ivy pushed her brother's hand away, adding, "—and

magic! And *mad science*! And the *super-secret and sinister history of our town's founders*!"

"None of that is even real, Ivy," Linus said. "Well—except for the part about the strange history of East Emerson."

"What are you talking about?" Will asked. "What strange history?"

"Should we tell him?" Ivy asked her brother with a smile.

Linus returned her smile. "Better to *show* him."

Dear Reader, do you have friends? I hope you do. Friends are good for many things, such as telling jokes, sharing secrets, and of course, helping to educate you about things you don't know about. I once befriended a leopard who was very knowledgeable about how to survive in the deadly heat of the African desert. I also befriended a 4,845-year-old Great Basin bristlecone pine—which is a tree—in California who was very astute, especially in ways of keeping skin young. Of course, making friends with humans is much harder than animals and trees. Animals and trees are lovely. Humans? Not so much.

Whether Will Hunter knew it or not, he was well on his way to becoming friends with Ivy and Linus. And as such, these two were about to teach him about East Emerson's biggest secret—its secret history.

After school, Ivy and Linus walked Will toward the center of town. Along the way, they passed a Zamzummim walking a Ziz on a leash, a Zennyo Ryūō and a Zin battling a Zahhāk and a Zhū Què, and Zeus sharing ziti with a Zilant. Now, Zany Reader, I'm sure your first instinct is to think I'm making up words, but I am not. A Zamzummim is a giant and a Ziz is a griffin-like bird. A Zennyo Ryūō is a rain-making dragon, a Zin is a water spirit, a Zahhāk is a wicked dragon, and a Zhū Què is a fire elemental bird. Zeus, I'm sure you know as the king of Greek gods and a ziti is a pleasant pasta dish, while a Zilant is a flying chicken-legged dragon. Will began to wonder if he and his mom had somehow driven into a comic book or a movie rather than a new town.

"Come on, slow poke!" Ivy said, dragging Will toward the public library.

But Will hesitated as he stared up at the building that looked more like a haunted museum than a house of books. The entire structure looked as if it had been transported here from ancient Greece, with massive columns and a triangular roof. A few of the serpents carved into the marble stairs seemed to watch Will's each step.

"Why are we coming here? I need to find my dog," Will protested.

"Just come on. You can hang some more fliers inside—*after* we show you the good stuff," Ivy said.

This library was far bigger than the one at school. The pleasant smell of old books filled the giant quiet space. A few people milled about, browsing the colorful spines, while others sat reading.

When they got to the counter, Linus waved to the librarian. On a giant serpent tail, she slid all the way across the library in seconds. Like the school librarian, she was a lamia. "Linusss. What a pleasssant sssurprissse."

"Hello, Ms. Delphyne. This is Will Hunter, a new resident requiring introduction to East Emerson. I was hoping I might show him my favorite tome in the archive section. Would that be acceptable?"

"Of coursse, dear," Ms. Delphyne said with a smile—until she saw Ivy. "I trust that your sssissster didn't bring any food or beveragesss thisss time?"

"Nope!" Ivy said, showing both hands empty. "I learned my lesson. Promise not to touch anything."

"Good," Ms. Delphyne said. She slithered ahead of the trio to a doorway at the back of the library. She pulled a key on a chain from around her neck and unlocked the door. "Let me know if you need any asssissstance, Linusss. Otherwissse, lock up when you're done, pleassse."

"Of course," Linus said, with a polite bow. His eyes lingered on her as she slithered away.

Will noticed. "Linus, how would you describe Ms. Delphyne?"

Linus pushed his glasses up his nose. "Physically? A redheaded female in her early thirties who dresses in classic button-up sweaters and '70s-era glasses. Spiritually? I think it's safe to say she is a saint. All librarians are. They are keepers of information, guardians of atheneums."

The three climbed a staircase of old wooden steps, each creaking underfoot as if speaking to them. Will whispered to Ivy, "Does he know, you know, that the librarian is a lamia?"

"Lamia? Is that what they're called?" Ivy asked. "I always called them snake-ladies."

"Ivy, how many times have I told you that Ms. Delphyne is *not* a snake-lady!" Linus snapped.

"I'm not saying *snake-lady* to be mean. She actually *is* a snake-lady," Ivy said.

"Lamia," Will corrected.

"Was that in your monster comics too?"

"Actually, a video game," Will said. "So she's not... dangerous?"

"Nah. All the lamias in town are pretty chill. They work at the libraries and the bookstores. They don't even eat children anymore."

"How do you know?" Will asked.

Ivy smirked. "I like to eavesdrop."

"*Shhhhh!*" Linus commanded. "A little respect please."

Ivy elbowed Will in the ribs. "My little brother *loves* libraries—like he's *in love* with them."

"You say that like it's a bad thing," Linus noted. "A library is a repository of knowledge. It houses millions of voices from past, present, and future literary geniuses and scholars. Not to mention, you can discover the truth of any historical battle or scientific principle here."

"Isn't that what the internet is for?" Ivy asked.

"Certainly, the World Wide Web is an equitable resource, and search engines are useful for more recent information," Linus explained, "but to truly delve into history, you'll find there is something special—primal even—about hunting through musty archives and truly working to discover the truth."

"Yeah, no," Ivy said. "I prefer the easy route."

Linus led Ivy and Will through the tall stacks of the library's attic. The books here were larger and older than those downstairs. Many of the volumes were leather bound, their pages thick and yellow, some appearing as old as dinosaurs.

The far wall was covered in weapons: sabers, scabbards, scimitars, scythes, swords, and shields, alongside sgian-dubh, shotel, sica, sikin panyang, sovnya, spatha, stiletto, surik, and a susuwat. "Why are their weapons in the library?" Will asked.

Linus scoffed. "Books are hardly weapons."

Will looked at Ivy, who mouthed, *He can't see them, which I'm guessing means they're magic*.

Will shook it off. "So the lamia, *urm*, I mean, librarian just lets kids up here?"

"Certainly not." Linus smiled. "She lets *me* up here. I've been coming here since I was four. Ms. Delphyne knows me and my utmost respect for all books. I spend dawn to dusk here most weekends, reading about various disciplines. That is how I found this treasured tome."

Linus took them through a keyhole-shaped door into a small back room. There, the only light came in through the only window—a triangle stained glass displaying a serpent spiraling into the center. The red glass cast a red light across a large table, the only furniture in the room. On it lay a massive, ancient book, protected under a glass box. Gently, Linus raised the glass, then leaned over and inhaled. As if he were smelling a dozen fresh cookies, a smile appeared on his face. He raised the first half of the book as gently as he might carry a newborn baby, to show Will the cover. In a strange old font, it read: *PERDITIT HISTORIA RERUM*.

"It's Latin for 'the history of lost things,'" Linus translated. He thumbed through the thick, massive pages until he found the what he was looking for. It was a map spread across two pages. "Recognize anything?"

Will noticed the curling tip of Massachusetts, and the island at its tip. "It looks like here. I mean, the island of East Emerson, only like a hundred years ago."

"Try *twelve hundred* years ago," Linus explained. "According to this date in the corner, this map was drawn in 827 AD."

Will was confused. "But America wasn't discovered until 1492 by Columbus. Right?"

Linus shook his head with a knowing grin. "Indigenous Americans discovered the Americas around fifteen thousand years ago. European countries didn't start coming to this country until about six hundred years ago. But according to this book, there were other visitors two hundred years before the turn of the tenth century."

Ivy went to turn the page, but Linus slapped her hand away. "Only *I* touch the book."

Softly, he turned the next page. There was a long entry, written in strange writing. "More Latin, which is odd," Linus explained, "considering this part of the book was written by a man claiming to be a *Viking* named Emer the Red. From what little I've translated, he claims to be a Norse explorer who discovered this land with Artemis, a witch who would one day become his wife."

"So you're saying Vikings came to East Emerson?"

"They came and stayed, along with two hundred friends," Linus said. "They settled here. According to this book, there was an entire village."

"And?"

"Then they vanished." Linus turned page after page, until the entries stop. After, there were the tatters of where pages had been ripped out, leaving only one page with a single word:

JÖRMUNGANDR

Will, Ivy, and Linus stared at one another in silence. Little did the friends know that all three of them experienced a cold chill running up their spines at the exact same moment.

"That word," Will said. "It's carved into the tree in the cemetery. What's it mean?"

"It's on my list of things to research," Linus said, "which unfortunately is a rather long list. And schoolwork is always my priority."

"See? It's not just people's *pets* that vanish in this town," Ivy said. "It's *people* too. An entire group of Vikings vanished without a trace."

"Not 'without a trace,'" Linus said. "There's this book. But no, no explanation of what happened to them after."

"You're freaking me out," Will said. "Are you telling

me East Emerson is built on the same spot as an ancient Viking village that went missing?"

"That is correct," Linus answered.

Ivy shook her head. "And no one thought that was a bad idea? Whoever founded this town was a bunch of grade A morons."

"Unless they did it on purpose for some nefarious reason," Linus added. "Hypothetically speaking of course."

"What's that?" Will asked. The corner of a weathered piece of pink paper stuck out from beneath the book. Linus carefully pulled it out. It was a handwritten note.

If asking where
I'd suggest the
pet store collar
wherever that was,
If you Go
up or down.
Do not Follow
or else the
night swallows shadows.

"It's nonsense," Linus said.

"No, it's a code," Will said to Ivy. "Like that note you passed me in class."

"That's creepy," Ivy said. "That note was the first time I used that code."

"So someone knew about the code *and* about Fitz's collar. That means—" Will's voice lowered "—they wanted *us* to find this."

Ivy shivered. "That's even creepier."

"But who wrote this? What's it have to do with Fitz? And does it have something to do with all the monsters in town?"

"Not you too," Linus moaned.

Will decided to just come clean. "Linus, I know it sounds impossible, but Ivy's telling the truth. I *see* stuff, stuff that no one else does, except Ivy because she has a ring that lets her see it too."

Linus took off his glasses and pinched his nose. "Is she *paying* you to prank me? How much?"

"No, we're telling the truth," Will said. "Ivy, give him your ring, so he can see the librarian for what she really is."

Ivy rolled her eyes. "Wow, simple solution, Will. Wish

I'd thought of that," Ivy moaned sarcastically. "I've tried that. The ring only works for me."

"Wait—you mean the ring your birth parents left you?" Linus asked.

Ivy shoved her ring hand into her pocket, as if suddenly uncomfortable. Then she barked at Linus, "I'm not lying, dude. You have to trust me."

"Trust is difficult with you. You lie to teachers to get out of exams," Linus noted.

"Okay, well, I don't lie to family," Ivy corrected herself.

"Yes, you do! The other day, Dad made oatmeal chocolate chip walnut cookies for me and you ate all of them, then lied about it!"

"Dad made those cookies for both of us. And I didn't eat them!" Ivy yelled back. "The Flelfs did!"

"No, Dad said he was proud of me for acing my biology exam, and thus he made cookies."

"Yeah, but he was proud of me for acing hockey practice. Plus, I'm his favorite."

"Dad doesn't have favorites. He says so often."

"Then why does he buy me fireworks?" Ivy asked.

"*Dad* is the culprit supplying you with those dangerous incendiary devices?!"

"Enough!" Will shouted, stepping between the arguing brother and sister. He didn't know why he was shouting, except that his heart was pounding in his chest and his head was cloudy. "I just want to find my dog! Why did you even bring me here?"

"To tell you about the town history," Linus whispered. "I find it truly fascinating. I thought it might take your mind off your worries."

"I brought you here because I think there's a connection," Ivy said. "Think about it! All those Vikings disappeared way back when, and now animals are going missing left and right. Don't you think there's a connection?"

"No, no, I don't," Will said. His mind was flooded with information. All the monsters, the Vikings, this weird book, his arguing neighbors, Fitz missing—maybe gone forever? Suddenly, Will felt like he couldn't breathe.

He rushed out of the attic, down the steps, through the library, and outside. He ran across the street into the town center. He raced across the grass, then braced himself against the gazebo, trying to catch his breath and calm his pounding heart. The whole world was spinning.

He wanted to cry and scream and run away and disappear, all at the same time.

Linus and Ivy appeared behind him. They approached slowly. "Will, are you okay?"

"I… I…can't breathe," Will said, on the verge of tears. He didn't want to cry. That'd be so embarrassing. "I think I'm having a heart attack. I feel like I'm going crazy."

"Is it possible you are having a panic attack?" Linus asked gently. "Often when I am overcome with anxiety, I feel like I might perish. But feelings are not facts. That's what my therapist says.

"Just breathe," Linus said. "Inhale and count to three. Then exhale and do the same."

Will breathed slowly.

"Keep going," Linus said.

Will did it. He felt the world stop spinning. He was still scared, but more, he felt ashamed. He whispered, "I'm sorry I freaked out…"

"It's cool. I freak out all the time," Ivy said. "That's why our parents ask us to go to therapy once a month. They think I'm dealing with adoption issues. But really it's just the monster stuff."

"I do not see monsters," Linus said, pushing his glasses

up his nose, "though I do suffer from anxiety. The world can be a very stressful place."

"No kidding," Will whispered. "So you don't think I'm a total weirdo?"

"You are certainly no weirder than my sister," Linus stated with a small smile.

Ivy playfully punched Linus's arms. But the siblings smiled.

"And here I thought you were Mr. Cool," Ivy said. "Nice to know you're just like the rest of us...weirdos."

"You thought *I* was cool?" Will asked, surprised.

"Yeah. I mean, you moved from New York City. That's pretty cool."

Will felt his face blush.

"Are you feeling better?" Linus asked.

"A little. Yeah. I just... I can't shake this feeling. Ever since I moved here... I don't know. And with Fitz gone, this one thought keeps popping into my head. Back in Brooklyn, on the Fourth of July, people would set off fireworks, and it drove Fitz bonkers. He even ran away a few times. What if...what if all the animals in East Emerson are running away because they instinctively know something terrible and dangerous is coming?"

"Like what?" Ivy asked. "Wait—what if all of East Emerson is going to vanish? Like with the Vikings?"

Linus shook his head. "Unlikely. Obviously, I do not believe a word of this mystical, magical mumbo-jumbo nonsense. I am a man of science and fact. That said, if the two of you *are* telling the truth—which you clearly are *not*—then I might hypothesize that East Emerson is some kind of nexus point, a convergence for all the weird the world has to offer. Perhaps the supernatural is drawn here to an object or being of great power that we do not know of. Perhaps that supernatural element was the cause of the Vikings' disappearance, and perhaps something in the same vein is now repeating itself. Of course, that's all about as likely as me becoming a witch one day."

"Don't you mean wizard?" Ivy asked.

Linus rolled his eyes. "I do not believe in heteronormative gender roles and stereotypes. A man can be a witch just as easily as a woman."

"My first night here," Will recalled, "there was a witch and a silver fox. And the fox said, 'Save the animals, and save the town.' Now I have to save Fitz. Do you think it's all connected?"

"It has to be," Ivy whispered. "I mean that's a pretty

direct message. We save Fitz, and the other animals, we save the town."

"Now we just have to figure out *how*," Will whispered.

"OMG, a real-life adventure!" Ivy slapped her hands together in excitement. "I'm in. Let's do it. Let's solve all the mysteries of this town! We'll be heroes—and even better, I'll prove to everyone monsters are real!"

All Will could think about was Fitz. "If saving East Emerson means finding Fitz, I'm in too."

Linus pinched the bridge of his nose. "This is ridiculous."

"It's not ridiculous," Ivy said, pulling her brother's ear. "It's magic and monsters and—"

"—*myth and mad science*. Yes, yes, I know your spiel," Linus noted. "But those things do *not* exist. Well, perhaps mad science—though science cannot truly be *mad*, so much as morally dishonorable at times, depending on the scientist. Whatever the case, I am positive there is a rational explanation for what you two *think* you're seeing. So I suppose I will be joining your little expedition, to find out the true facts."

"Are we really doing this?" Ivy asked, a twinkle in her

eye. “Are we going to uncover the heart of the darkness in East Emerson?”

“It appears so,” Linus stated. “Where do we start?”

Ivy held up the pink note from the library. “We follow our clue.”

Will smiled. “Fitz, hang in there. I’m coming for you.”

Chapter 7

Eight Legs Underground

✶

The Saturday morning sun was rising in a blue sky as Will, Ivy, and Linus rode their bikes down the dirt road toward the crumbling Svengali Fairgrounds.

Looking over at Ivy and Linus, Will couldn't help but smile. Riding bikes with friends reminded him of warm summer days when he and Marcellus would spend entire afternoons riding around Brooklyn or across the bridges into Manhattan. East Emerson had green trees and rolling hills instead of honking cabs and sky-bound buildings, but the feeling was the same.

As Linus took the lead, Ivy nodded to Will. "Hey. I'm still wondering, if you don't have a ring, how do you see the stuff I do?"

"I've been thinking about it too," Will admitted, "and still no idea."

"Have you ever seen supernatural stuff before?"

Will shook his head. "Only in video games and movies and comics. I've always been drawn to fantasy, but I never believed in it. I guess maybe I hoped it was real, but until I came to East Emerson, it never was."

"Maybe you're cursed," Ivy said.

"Actually, that would make a lot of sense," Will mumbled to himself, thinking of his life. "So...how about your ring? Why do you wear it? You could take it off, and just be, you know...normal."

Ivy whispered, "It's the only thing my birth parents left me. I don't know anything about them—except that they wanted me to have it. When I wear it... I dunno... I feel closer to them. Does that make any sense?"

Will thought of Fitz, who was a gift from his dad. He needed to find Fitz, not just because he loved his dog, but because Fitz was a connection to happier times. Fitz made Will feel like Dad was still around. "It makes perfect sense."

Ivy sniffed. "Anyway. Being normal is overrated. I like being different."

"No one likes being different," Linus interjected, having slowed his bike to join the conversation.

"I do," Ivy said. "Who wants to be just like everyone else?"

Will and Linus exchanged a shared glance. Will was the first to admit, "I wouldn't mind fitting in with everybody. It's nice to belong."

Linus added, "The human being is a social animal by nature. We require the recognition and acceptance that can only be provided by our peers."

"Whatever." Ivy charged ahead, not looking back.

Linus shook his head. "I love my sister, but she does prefer being contrary to being honest."

The trio parked their bikes at the abandoned park entrance. Once again, Will found himself staring up at the giant clown statues holding up the sign.

Linus took one look at the sign and said, "Seriously, Ivy? Defacement of private property is a felony."

"Did I miss something?" Will asked.

Linus pointed to the handwritten word *disappear*. "That's my sister's handiwork."

Ivy giggled, pulling a thick black Sharpie from her back pocket.

"You wrote that?" Will asked.

Ivy smirked. "Guilty as charged. But come on, no one cares about this place."

"You wrote on the Welcome to East Emerson sign too, didn't you?"

Ivy shrugged. "I thought we were here to explore. Come on."

As Ivy walked between the giant clowns holding the marquee, Will shivered. "Maybe we shouldn't do this. I told you I was almost attacked here. By clowns."

"Don't be a chicken," Ivy said. "It's only an amusement park—just old and abandoned!"

Just old and abandoned? Dreaded Reader, that's like saying, oh, it's only a *haunted* house. Have you ever seen a place that is abandoned? Whether it's a factory, or a school, or an old hospital, you'll find that it presents an uncomfortable feeling in your gut. Some say, "It gives me the willies!" or "It gives me the creeps!" or "Oh, god, please make the screaming stop!" Whatever people say, heed my advice: beware abandoned places. Sure, maybe it's only that things look sad when no one loves them anymore—myself included—but in my experience, fear is information. Do not ignore it…

"Ivy. There are monsters here," Will whispered.

"There are monsters everywhere," Ivy said.

"Certainly not. But this is where the note told us to go," Linus said, adjusting the straps on his giant backpack.

Will's stomach churned, doing somersaults. He tried to focus on happy things—like his *MonsterWorld* comics, his mom, and Fitz. It also helped that it was several hours until the sun set. Plus, Dear Reader, Will was not alone this time. When one is with friends, you often find yourself stronger and braver. Strength in numbers, I suppose.

"Fine. For Fitz," Will said. "But at the first sign of clowns, we run. Okay?"

"But what if they want to make us balloon animals?" Ivy asked.

"Balloons are bad for the environment," Linus noted.

Will ignored them. "This way. I found Fitz's collar by the entrance of a ride called the Cave of Doom."

"Hey, I've been there! Dad brought us before the park closed for good," Ivy said. "It's basically a real underground cave. You just walk through it, and stuff jumps out and scares you."

"I recall it as well," Linus noted. "It was a rather crude attempt at frightening children."

"It worked on you," Ivy said, nudging her brother.

"When the giant plastic spider dropped down from the ceiling, you totally peed yourself."

"No, I spilled my beverage on myself. The trickery was crude but no less effective." Linus adjusted his glasses. "And mind you, I was five years old."

"Why did the park close?" Will asked.

"A bunch of teenagers snuck in here after hours," Ivy said. "They wanted to ride the Metal Monsoon roller coaster. Only they didn't know it was broken. They went off the tracks. That was the end of their joyride."

"Their guardians sued the fairgrounds owners, who then went bankrupt. The park shut its doors permanently," Linus said. "Terrible tragedy."

"Agreed," Ivy said. "The amusement park was the one thing East Emerson had going for it."

"I meant the loss of life," Linus said.

"Yeah, that too," Ivy said.

"So this Cave of Doom," Will started, "if it's a real cave, maybe that's where the note wants us to go. It said, to go down and follow the shadows."

"You said the storm that chased you was made up of bats and birds and stuff, right? Well, Fitz may have chased one down there. You saw how he freaked out over the hare with wings."

"For Fitz," Will repeated, his nerves frayed. He took a deep breath as he led the way. He was relieved to see the old park was clown-free today—until he turned a corner. Will shrieked, *"A Clown! Run!!"*

Ivy grabbed him by the belt before he got too far, saying, "Chill! It's just a painting on the wall. Are you really that afraid of clowns?"

"No!" Will lied. "I just think we need to be careful. Keep our eyes peeled for anything suspicious—"

The trio hesitated at the mouth to the Cave of Doom. Though it was bright and sunny outside, it was pitch-black inside the stairwell that led down into the cave. They couldn't see more than a few feet into the darkness. Will asked, "Who wants to go into the dark scary cave first?"

Linus gulped. "There is nothing to fear. Dark is only the absence of light. I would volunteer, but I wear glasses, thus proving my eyesight is far from adequate. Might I recommend someone with twenty-twenty vision?"

Will wondered if the clowns might be hiding down there. "Well, uh, maybe we should go get an adult? I think that's a pretty good idea."

Ivy rolled her eyes at both guys. "Since I'm the bravest, I'll go." She walked straight into the darkness and disappeared down the stairs.

"Hey! I'm brave too!" Will said. He grabbed the railing and stumbled down into the darkness.

"Can you see anything?" Ivy asked.

"I can't even see my nose," Will said. When they reached the bottom floor of the cave, the air was cooler. It smelled of earth and water. "Linus?"

There was nothing but silence in the pitch black. Will and Ivy turned around in circles, but could see nothing. "Linus?"

A bright light flashed in the darkness. Will and Ivy screamed, grabbing one another as shields. Linus lowered his flashlight with a smirk. "Why am I not surprised you two came into a cave without thinking of an illumination mechanism first?"

"Leave it to my brother, the nerd-burger, to have a flashlight in his backpack," Ivy snorted. "He has everything in there—except the kitchen sink."

"There is nothing wrong with attending an exploration well prepared," Linus said. He lay his backpack down and unzipped it. He flashed his light over it so Will could see. Every inch of space was packed with something useful.

He retrieved a second flashlight and handed it to Will. "And why would I have a kitchen sink? There is no need for it on our expedition."

"It was a joke," Ivy said. But before her brother zipped up the backpack, she reached in and grabbed a plastic bag. "Oooh! Gummy worms!"

While Ivy chomped loudly, Will and Linus took the lead. The flashlights revealed the passage was a real cave, but one that had been laid with mechanical traps to scare people. A rickety, rusted metal rail marked the wandering path. Around each corner or rock were the dusty recreations of old movie monsters—Dracula, Frankenstein, a mummy, an invisible man, a werewolf. Behind those were systems of wires and pulleys that once controlled their ability to jump out. The next stretch had swooping torn sheets to act as ghosts and granite walls painted with murals of goblins, phantoms, and other ghoulish creatures. Not long after, the trio came to a large room, but the next passage was barred with a metal fence.

Linus noted, "We have discovered a dead end."

"Do you have to say 'dead'?" Will mumbled. "Wait, did you hear that?"

"The only thing I hear is my sister smacking," Linus noted.

Ivy burped in her brother's ear. "Did you hear *that*?"

"Rude," Linus muttered. "Chew like your mouth has a secret."

"*Shhhh*. Seriously, I heard something," Will whispered. He took the flashlight and swept the cavernous room made to look like an archaic laboratory. Overhead, giant stalactites hung down from the ceiling like monstrous teeth. Perched on sandstone shelves and old tables were bottles and aquariums of bizarre beasts suspended in murky liquid, including a two-headed horse and an adult-sized amphibious creature.

Otherwise, the three sleuths were alone. So why did Will feel like someone was watching them?

Linus flashed his light around a new bend. "Observe—a service entrance."

"The grate's pulled open," Ivy noted. Fearlessly, she hopped through the opening to examine the other side. "Whoever did this must be strong as heck. I bet it was a *giant*."

"Yet another implausible leap in logic," Linus said.

"Any person could bend bars using applied force and instruments such as a crowbar or winch."

Ivy guided her brother's flashlight over. "I don't think crowbars or winches leave indented handprints."

"I do not see what you see," Linus said.

Ivy groaned. "Of course not."

Skritch. Skritch-skritch.

"Okay, did you hear *that*?" Will whispered. Ivy and Linus both nodded.

Skritch-skritch. Skritch-skritch. The sounds echoed through the caverns. Will and Linus joined Ivy on the other side of the hole in the gate, hiding behind a rock.

The three friends sat there, waiting, hearts pounding in their chests. They pounded so loudly, Dear Reader, that you might be able to hear them now if you listen hard enough. *Shhh!* Listen...

Do you hear that?

Oh wait, that's *my* heartbeat. No, wait...

...that's *your* heartbeat.

You're scared, aren't you? Good. I mean, don't be. Doomed Reader, you have my word that *at least* two of the children in this story will survive their first adventure.

"Turn off the lights," Ivy hissed. "Don't make a sound."

The three huddled behind the rock in silence. As their eyes adjusted to the darkness, they could just make out the faint light coming from the entrance. *Skritch-skritch.* As the sounds came closer, two long shadows appeared at the end of the corridor, lumbering this way. Whatever they were, their footsteps sounded large and scratchy. *Skritch-skritch. Skritch-skritch.*

"What are they?" Will whispered. "Giants? Yetis? Bigfoots?"

"I believe the plural of Bigfoot would be *Bigfeet*," Linus whispered, "which also, do *not* exist."

Ivy wrapped her hand over her brother's mouth.

Skritch-skritch. Skritch-skritch. Skritch-skritch. Skritch-skritch.

Will leaned forward, squinting to see—until he lost his balance and fell forward, his flashlight leaping from his hand. It turned on when it hit the floor, spinning light all over the cavern as it flew across the floor. The revolving light flashed on the intruders: two whip spiders towering twelve feet tall, their hind legs raking against the ceiling. The eight-eyed, eight-legged creatures were pale brown with mandibles stretching out five feet away. At the site of the light, and Will, Ivy, and Linus, the spiders screeched a horrific, hungry cry. They charged forward.

Ivy grabbed Linus's flashlight and screamed, "Spiders! Run!"

Will and Linus sped after Ivy, as she ran down the service corridor with the flashlight bouncing all around. They dodged more fake ghosts made of torn fabric as well as plastic goblins bolted to rusted machinery. Behind them, they could hear the spiders ripping the gate apart, trying to get in. There was a loud metal crash, and then the sound of long legs rushing down the hall. *Skritch-skritch-skritch-skritch.*

Will, Ivy, and Linus crashed into a giant spiderweb. They all screamed, but no one as loud as Linus who was shrieking breathlessly. Will realized first that they weren't stuck to it. "It's not real..." he gasped, trying to catch his own breath. "Just another prop... Keep running!"

But as the three friends looked around for an exit, they found none. The service corridor ended at a locked door.

Skritch-skritch-skritch-skritch-skritch-skritch. The spiders were getting closer.

Will tried the doorknob. No luck. He slammed his

body into the old door. Ivy joined him. They both threw their bodies into the door. Nothing. It was made of metal and wouldn't budge. "There has to be another way out!"

Skritch-skritch-skritch-skritch-skritch-skritch. The long-legged creatures turned the corner, their thin legs entering the tunnel before them as they tried to squeeze through the low ceiling. One of the spider's paws stretched forward, raking at Linus's shoe.

"I don't want to be spider food!" Linus cried out. "I can't die like this! Not spiders! Anything but spiders!"

Ivy yanked her brother back. The three of them pressed themselves to the back wall, but the spider's legs were too long. They were getting closer. Barely an inch away.

Then the sound of granite sliding against granite raked their ears. A hidden door opened on the wall to their left, between them and the spiders.

A deep, gruff voice said, "YOU SHOULDN'T BE HERE ALONE."

An eight-foot-tall figure climbed out of a hidden door in the ground. A mess of black hair and beard covered the man's face. His whole body was made of muscle, like some mythic beast or a comic superhero. Will stared at the man's hands and face, at the sickly gray skin, as though he were—

The spiders smashed through the rock and barreled toward them.

The bearded man held the rock slab door open, bellowing, "THROUGH HERE. HURRY."

"Don't have to tell me twice." Ivy grabbed Linus and shoved him through in first, then leaped in after.

Will hesitated. "Who are you?"

Their eyes met. The stranger had one emerald eye and one yellow, the color of a snake stripe.

As the spiders attacked, the bearded man punched one with his giant fist. He growled, "GO!"

The spiders swiped at Will with thorny mandibles. The stranger shielded Will, taking the brunt of the spiders' attack, their teeth slicing through his arm. Will wanted to help, but he didn't know how. Before he could do or say anything, the gray man roared, "ESCAPE THROUGH THE TUNNELS. DO NOT COME BACK FOR ME." He pushed Will through the trapdoor, into the darkness, then slammed the door behind him.

Will tumbled down a long staircase, until he crashed onto the floor next to Ivy and Linus.

"Please remove your bodies from my person," Linus squeaked from the bottom of the pile.

"He saved us, and we don't even know who he is..." Will whispered.

"Saved us? He threw us into a pitch-black cellar and locked us in," Ivy groaned. "He's probably going to eat us after he's done with the spiders."

"No, he wanted us to escape," Will said. He thought of the kindness—and the sadness—in the bearded stranger's eyes. He shined his flashlight around the room. The light flickered for a second. "And we're not in a cellar. It's a tunnel. Look."

Linus was still shaking. "Why did it have to be arachnids?"

"What's an arachnid?" Ivy asked.

"The class of eight-legged invertebrates you call spiders."

"Wait, you saw the giant spiders?!" Ivy asked.

"I...did not," Linus confessed. "I have an unwavering phobia of arachnids. As soon as you screamed 'Spiders!' I ran. I do not need to see them to know I am deathly afraid."

"Dude, they were no joke like twelve feet tall!"

"That is unlikely," Linus said, adjusting his glasses,

"as well as a terrifying idea. The largest known spider is a male goliath bird-eating spider found in Venezeula—which is nowhere close to here—and even it is only eleven inches long. Hardly bigger than a dinner plate. Perhaps you're thinking of the Amblypygi, also known as the cave-dwelling whip spider. Some of those can be as long as twenty-eight inches."

"If you're so afraid, how do you know so much about them?" Ivy asked.

"I find that facing my phobias through education is a...way to help understand my fear and hopefully one day reconcile it," Linus said.

"How's that working for you?" Ivy asked.

"Not great," Linus stated.

Ivy swatted Linus. He swatted her back. The two siblings started swatting in rapid fire.

Above, the sounds of the fight between the bearded man and the spiders quieted away, as if moving into the distance. Will climbed the stairs to the stone door. He listened for a minute, then tried to push it open. It wouldn't move. It was way too heavy.

"We need to go back and help him," Will called out.

"No. We need to find a way out of here," Ivy said. "That

guy saved us, which *hey, awesome and thank you*, but he told us to escape. If he sacrificed himself, he doesn't want us sticking around, waiting for those spiders to come back. I say we get out of here."

"I am inclined to agree with Ivy. Better safe than sorry," Linus said.

Will didn't want to leave, but he was outvoted. And he was scared. Before he turned to leave, he noted the door was marked with three lines:

III

With the flashlight, Will led the way into the tunnel.

"This place looks man-made," Ivy noted. "Think this is part of the amusement park?"

"Unlikely. These tunnels are far older by the looks of it," Linus said, studying the wall. "The stones comprising the walls have been in place for decades, if not longer. You can tell by the moss growth and the water marks created over an extensive period of time."

Will traced his fingers along the wall, which was as cold and damp as the air. The corridor was perfectly round. "Maybe they're part of the town's sewer system?"

"Great," Ivy said. "So if someone flushes above us, we're gonna get *gross*."

"I think not," Linus said. "This is not a sewage duct. No labels, no numbers, no pipes. This tunnel is far older. But how is that possible? Who would have built it, and why?"

"Maybe the underground lizard people built it," Ivy suggested.

"There is no such thing," Linus growled.

"There is," Ivy insisted. "I've seen them."

As the siblings argued, Will shined the flashlight and traced his fingers along the wall. Parts were covered in moss and slime. But up ahead he noticed a cleared patch with more writing—just like he and Ivy had discovered on the mouth of the well in the cemetery. Carved into the stones read:

← GSV UZRITILFMWH

GSV ULIVHG ZMW GSV NLFMGZRM NRMVH →

"Great. More gibberish," Will said.

Ivy pointed to the arrows. "I bet they're directions. Too bad we don't know how to decipher the code."

Will's flashlight flickered. Then the glow dimmed.

He smacked it against his palm. The light stuttered, then went out.

"Not funny, Will," Ivy said. "Turn the flashlight on."

"It wasn't me!" Will said. He slapped and shook the flashlight. Nothing.

Ivy snorted. "*Aaaand* we're lost in the dark. What do we do now?"

"Do you have any batteries in your pack?"

Linus hesitated before admitting, "No."

"But you're supposed to be Mr. Prepared!" Ivy snapped.

"I have a limited allowance," Linus snapped back.

"Stay together," Will said. He grabbed Ivy's shoulder and Linus's backpack. "As long as we stick together and keep cool heads—"

Linus started screaming. *"Help!! Somebody help us please! I do not want to die in the dark!"* His cries echoed back and forth through the tunnel, on and on, until they seemed like someone was whispering it back to them from far away.

"Not helpful," Ivy said.

"I apologize," Linus said. "It was a temporary emotional reaction. I am fine now."

"Are you?"

"No," Linus said.

"This isn't good," Ivy said.

"This is bad," Will added.

"We are lost. In the dark. Potentially, never to see the sun again," Linus whispered, his voice quivering.

Ivy hugged her brother. "We'll get out of here. We just need to think."

"Do either of you have a cell phone?" Will asked.

"I wish," Ivy groaned. "Our parents won't let us have one. And it's so stupid. Every kid has a cell phone these days, but our parents are all, 'If you have a phone, you'll be on it all the time.' Or, 'You can't have a phone until you're sixteen.' Or, 'Ivy, give me my phone back this instant!'"

"Our parental units have been very anti–cell phone since Ivy ran up a two-thousand-dollar bill gambling on online sports," Linus explained.

"I thought it was a video game," Ivy said in defense. "But seriously. Every kid should have a cell phone for this exact type of situation—so we have games to play or a movie to watch during emergencies."

"Or for calling for help," Linus noted.

"Oh. That's smart too," Ivy said.

Will felt the darkness tugging at him, as if he would be trapped there forever. He tried to stay calm, but his heart raced. What if he never saw daylight again? What if he never saw his mom again? What if the shadow swarm was down here, and was hungry? And where was Fitz? Was the note a trap?

Will leaned against the tunnel wall for support, and he felt it. *Buh-bum. Buh-bum. Buh-bum. Buh-bum.*

"Do you feel that?" Will asked.

"What?" Ivy asked.

"Shhhh," Will hushed her. *Buh-bum. Buh-bum. Buh-bum. Buh-bum.*

"Are the spiders coming back?" Linus squeaked.

"No. It's a heartbeat," Will said. "Like the one Ivy and I heard at the well in the cemetery."

"That's miles away," Ivy said. "Do you think these tunnels are connected? If we start walking, we might be able to find a way out."

"Or we might get even more lost," Linus said.

"What has a heartbeat loud enough to fill an entire underground corridor?" Ivy asked.

"It is not a heartbeat. Perhaps it is a train, or electric conductors," Linus suggested.

"I don't care what it is," his sister said. "We need to get out of here, pronto."

"Then let's start walking," Will said. "But together."

Slowly, the three friends walked forward in the pitch black, holding on to one another like a three-caboose train. It felt like hours went by, but there was no telling without any light. They found fork after fork in the tunnels, and they kept going left, because they didn't know what else to do. But just as Will felt like the whole world would bury him down here, he saw a shimmer in the darkness.

He wasn't sure if it was something tiny close-up, or something large farther away. He walked toward it.

"Follow me," Will said. At first, Will thought his eyes were playing tricks on him. Then he recognized the soft glow as it got closer and the speck took shape. It had four legs and a tail, its coat made of moonlight.

The silver fox walked toward them. Will asked the others, "Are you seeing what I'm seeing?"

"Yes," Ivy whispered. "She's beautiful."

"I see nothing," Linus said, "only darkness."

The silver fox grew brighter as she approached, her paws padding along the tunnel. Ten feet away, she stopped. Her head tipped to the left, as if asking Will to follow. Then the fox turned around and began to trot away.

"She wants us to follow," Will said. "Come on."

Chapter 8

the witch in the woods

✷

"Where are we going?" Linus asked as he fumbled in the darkness.

"We're following a glowing silver fox," Ivy said.

"Foxes do not glow!" Linus crowed.

"This one does," Will said.

"I suppose," Linus started, "if there was some undiscovered and rare breed of Canidae that developed bioluminescence from evolving underground—"

But Will was not listening to Linus. Instead, he focused entirely on the fox's moonlike radiance. "Fox? What's happening? What is all this? Do you know where my dog is? I think you were trying to tell me something that night in the cemetery, but I don't understand any of it. Can't you just tell me what we need to do?"

The fox looked back, and seemed to shake her head. Will realized her shine began to fade. As the fox began to dim, Will saw another gleam in the black of the caves… a beam of sunlight, peeking in from somewhere above.

"A way out!" Ivy shouted.

She and Linus ran forward, passing Will and the fox. "Fox, wait—" he said, but the fox had already disappeared into the darkness. Will whispered to the void, "I just wanted to say thank you."

"I do not understand how you intuited our way through the pitch black, but I am grateful nonetheless," Linus called out to Will. "Though I'd be more grateful if you did not invent some grandiose ruse about mystical mammals to trick me."

Ivy rolled her eyes. "I don't know what a ruse is, but no one is tricking you, Linus. How many times do I have to tell you—you don't see what I see."

The siblings argued as Will joined them. He craned his neck to look up toward the blue sky. This arm of the tunnel ended here, at the bottom of a stone well—only the path to freedom was at least a hundred feet high and the walls were far too steep to climb. Will scanned the shaft for old ropes or vines or footholds to scale. There was nothing except more carvings in the walls. The first was a simple:

IV

"Ivy?" he whispered, wondering if that's what it meant. But then he looked at the carving below it:

GSV URIHG LU GSV 13
GL YIRMT NV GSV SVZW LU LIZXOV QLMVH
VZIMH Z YLMFH.

Deflated, Will leaned against a rock. It felt like every time he overcame one obstacle, there was another waiting for him. "How are we going to get out of here?"

As if in answer, an old rope ladder tumbled down from above.

"Ha!" Ivy said. "Ask and you shall receive. Linus, you go up first."

"Why must I precede you?" her brother asked.

"I was trying to be nice, butthead! Never mind." Ivy pushed Linus aside.

"Wait," Will said. "Who threw the rope down? Aren't you worried?"

"Nope." Ivy climbed. With each step, the rope ladder whined. "I'm thinking maybe one at a time on this thing. It's as old as...well, old folks."

Will and Linus watched as Ivy disappeared into the daylight. "Come on up," Ivy called. But there was a terrible scream as Ivy was yanked out of view.

"*IVY!*" Linus and Will shouted.

Will leaped onto the rope and climbed. Linus was just behind. As they neared the top, they didn't know what to expect. Will hoped whomever—or *what*ever—it was, they could overwhelm them with numbers, three to one. That is, if there was only *one* thing to fight.

"We're coming, sister!!" Linus shouted. "Hold on!!"

There was no reply.

Will made it out of the well first. He raised his fists, ready for a fight. But he saw nothing strange in any direction. A few trees and shrubs spotted the area, and they were just west of the forest and the hills. But no monsters. And no Ivy. Will shouted, "Ivy!"

Linus crawled over the lip of the well and tumbled out. "Where is she?!"

"I don't know," Will said.

"We have to find her!" Linus's eyes were brimming with fear.

"IVY!!!" they both screamed.

A snort came from behind a nearby bush. Then, *"Bwa-hahahahahahaha!"* Will and Linus walked over to find Ivy rolling on her back, laughing so hard she could barely talk. "I…got you…so…good! You're both…so…gullible!"

"Not cool, Ivy," Will said.

Linus kicked his sister's leg. "You almost gave me a panic attack!"

"Tee-hee-hee. I thought it was a hoot and a half," an unfamiliar voice drawled from behind them.

The trio slowly turned. A woman was giggling. She wore a worn pair of cowboy boots, scabs on her knees, jean shorts, and a pearl-button plaid shirt with the sleeves rolled up. A fanny pack hung off the side of her bony waist, and a large gardening hat sat on her head. But when she raised her chin, they saw she wore her red hair in two thick braids, her face was spotted with freckles, and she looked at least eighty years old, but there was a kind of strength about her that made her seem decades younger.

The oddest thing though was the red paisley kerchief

bandana tied around her eyes, and the ring-tailed lemur sitting on top of her shoulder eating a green Granny Smith apple.

"Who are you?" Will asked.

"And where'd you come from?" Ivy added. "I was totally alone up here two seconds ago!"

"*Pshaw*! Ain't no one ever alone—not in this world. Or the next! And who d'ya think threw down that rope ladder? Ropes don't just appear when ya call 'em—not unless ya spell 'em too." The old woman cackled, a thick Southern twang in her voice, and her hands were covered in dirt, as though she'd been digging in the ground.

"How'd you know we were going to be down there?" Will asked.

"Who d'ya think left the note? Every third word, was I right?" The woman winked at Ivy and Will, then started to walk off. She waved for them to follow. "Come on now. No time for diddle-dawdlin'. We gotta drop by my house before I send ya on your way."

"Yeah, *no*. I am *not* going to a stranger's home," Linus stated.

"Child, please! If I wanted to harm y'all, I woulda left ya down in the well. Now, quit back-talkin' and get to walkin'."

"I like her," Ivy noted, following the blindfolded woman.

Linus looked to Will for support. But Will shrugged. "If the fox led us here, I bet it's for a reason." He followed the old woman too.

Not wanting to be left behind or alone, Linus trailed after the others. You see, Favored Reader, it is not ever fun to be left behind or alone. I have experience with both, and each is heartbreakingly melancholy. *Melancholy*, you see, means sad or sullen or morose or simply depressed. And it isn't just unhappy for me, but for you too, since you have to hear me whine and complain about it when I write.

Thankfully for you, I am a considerate and polite monster who will not bore you with the details of my time living alone in the crags and cliffs of Transylvania where I was desperately isolated, solitary, forsaken, and friendless, crying so much I might have filled a sea. No, you certainly do not want to hear of it. Especially not the part about meeting a great Wallachian prince nicknamed Vlad the Impaler and a beautiful British queen by the name of Victoria, which together, the three of us saved the world—or at least, all of Europe. But as I said, I am far too polite to bore you with that tale. Now, where were we? Oh, yes...

"What's your name?" Ivy asked the old woman.

"Jones. Oracle Jones." Despite her age, Oracle walked much faster than the kids, who struggled to keep up with the agile old woman.

"Oracle," Will asked, "how did you know that we'd be in the well?"

The woman half turned, pointed to the bandana over her eyes, and smiled. "I see the future."

Linus rolled his eyes.

"I saw that, kid," Oracle called out, hopping over a stone in her way. "Ya may not believe in such things, but time ain't nothing more than perception. Ya can see patterns if ya know where to look. Tossing bones, reading tea leaves, divination..."

"Any scientific verification to back up your claims?" Linus asked.

"Science is just another word for magic, deary," Oracle Jones laughed. "Hexes, experiments, potions, medicines, it's all the same when ya get down to it."

"Hexes and potions? You mean like witchcraft?" Ivy asked.

"Ain't no *like* about it, baby girl. The craft is the craft. I should know. I'm a witch."

Will stopped walking. "A witch?"

"Don't worry, kid. I'm on the side of the fox."

"You know her?" Will gasped. "The fox that glows like the moon?"

Linus snorted. "Here we go."

Oracle Jones pointed her freckled crooked finger directly at Linus. "That's strike two, kid! Mind that tone. Don't be judgin' things you ain't know nothin' about."

The lemur leaped from Oracle's shoulder to her head, then threw its apple core at Linus with a shriek. It bounced off Linus's chest and fell to his feet.

Linus huffed. "Fine. If you are a practitioner of witchcraft, *prove it*. Show us some magic."

"I ain't no sideshow..." she said. But then the right corner of her thin lips curled upward. "But fine. I'll show ya once. Keep them peepers peeled."

The old woman kneeled. She touched the earth, raised her hands to the air, then chanted between her palms, quieter than a whisper. When she opened her hands, a ball of blue energy formed there. She whispered to it, *"Crescere arbore pomum."*

The sparks grew, flowing into an enormous azure ring, spinning around the witch, creating a maelstrom of wind. Oracle cast her hands forward, and gusts bowled forward, knocking Linus, Ivy, and Will over. They got up to see the energy swirl into the apple core. It began to grow, taking root, growing into the ground, thickening, sprouting up toward the sky, unfurling limbs and leaves and seconds later, dozens of apples. The circle of blue energy burned to green, then vanished into a wisp of smoke.

"You made a tree," Will whispered. He touched the trunk, the leaves. It was real. Solid. Beautiful.

Ivy plucked an apple from a low branch and bit into it. "This is the best apple I've ever tasted," Ivy said. "Can you teach me how to do that?"

Linus gasped, as if seeing magic for the first time. But just as quickly, a kind of dull, unimpressed notion came over him. Like he'd forgotten what he'd just seen. He pinched the bridge of his nose. "What are you two talking about? *Nothing happened.*"

Ivy pointed. "Then where'd this apple tree come from?!"

"It was always there."

Oracle tapped Linus's glasses. "You ain't got the Sight?"

Linus swatted her hand away. "I can see just fine, thank you very much. I just don't see make-believe."

"What my annoying little brother means to say is, no, he can't see the good stuff," Ivy answered. "Just me and Will."

Oracle Jones burst into laughter. She laughed so hard, she doubled over, grabbing her belly. "Oh, lordy! Y'all's quest is gonna be a trip! Now, move y'all's feet. We have things to do..." She counted on her fingers as if trying to recall. "One, I was told I needed to talk to ya. Two, give ya gifts. Three, tell ya to find yourself a golden pyramid—"

"Like Egyptian pyramids?" Ivy asked.

"There are also pyramids in Mexico, Guatemala, Sudan, China—" Linus added.

"Don't interrupt!" Oracle snapped. "I got lots to do, and need to send ya home before sunset. Never good to be out after dark—not in this town."

Will jogged to catch up with the woman. "The silver fox—who is she?"

"Ain't my place to tell," Oracle said.

"What about the witch in the graveyard—tall, pale, purple hair? The fox wanted me to see her."

Oracle stopped, the smile fading from her face. "She's old evil. Gone by lots of different names through the centuries. These days, folks call her Oestre, Ozzie for short. Bad news, that one. Same as the twelve she runs with, callin' themselves The Thirteen. Ozzie's crew're behind everything bad brewing in East Emerson. Thirteen disciples of Chaos, searchin' for something sleeping underground, something best left alone..."

Oracle's thoughts seemed to drift off as her voice lowered until it was so quiet, Will could barely hear her say: "*...the seven of us didn't stand a chance against* him..."

The old woman shook it off. "Glad ya survived seeing Ozzie. Most don't. Y'all see her again? Run the other way. She ain't to be messed with."

"She's dangerous?" Ivy asked.

Oracle said, "She'll kill ya. She'll destroy anything that gets in her way."

"How do you know all of this?"

"There ain't much I don't see," Oracle said, her voice weighted down. "Means I know more than I'd like."

"Do you know why no one else can see what we can?" Will asked.

"There's a curse on this place. Ain't no one can see the supernatural truth—even when it's standin' right in front of them. Either folks see something normal or they ain't see nothin' at all. Makes East Emerson a safe haven for the mystical and the magical and all that. 'Course, most of them ain't bad. Just misunderstood. Not those Thirteen though. They got nothing but ill intentions."

"So how can *we* see?" Will asked.

"Either you learnt magic, or ya got a magic item."

"Is there a third option?"

"Not unless it's in your blood." Oracle Jones waved them off the worn path and into the woods.

As they passed between two giant trees with strange symbols carved into them, they suddenly found themselves in a massive yard with a house that hadn't been there a moment before. The garden was overgrown with wild weeds, volatile vines, bizarre and exotic flowers and cacti. The way was lined with hundreds of bodiless doll heads, each sitting on top of a stick shoved into the ground. All of the doll heads bobbled this way and that. No matter which way he stepped, hundreds of plastic eyes locked on to Will, as if watching him.

"Don't mind my dollies—they just keepin' them eyes on things." Oracle laughed to herself. Her lemur laughed with her.

A cloud of insects buzzed around them. As one landed on Will's arm, he prepared to slap it—until Oracle caught his wrist midair. "Look closer."

Will squinted at his arm, seeing the tiniest person ever dismount a mosquito with a saddle on its back. The miniscule man had gray-blue skin and wore strange armor. Will smiled. "Hey, little guy."

The man pulled a spear from his back and stabbed Will's arm. "*Ow!*"

"Watch out for forest sprites," Oracle noted. "They're nasty, mean little devils. Drink human blood like wine. Only takes a thimble-full to get 'em drunk."

"Forest sprites do not exist," Linus noted back. "These are mosquitoes from the family Culicidae." Linus slapped one buzzing at his neck.

As quick as a whip, Oracle Jones pinched Linus.

"*Ouch!*" he howled. "That hurt!"

"Then don't be hurtin' no livin' things on my property. They may look like bugs to ya, but those sprites have more right to be here in the Ever-Green than you or me."

Oracle waved the kids to follow her as she stepped up the creaking steps of her porch. Her ramshackle house looked a hundred years old, its yellow paint curling off in huge flecks like dead palm tree leaves. The whole structure leaned so far to the left, it appeared it might fall over if not braced by a giant willow tree.

When the witch got to her front door, she noticed several HOME FOR SALE picket signs leaning against the wall. A little too quickly, she kicked them over.

"You buying or selling houses?" Will asked, suspicious.

"It's a side hustle. Real estate is always a good investment," Oracle said. Then she waved them up the steps, "Come on in, now. We ain't got all day."

Linus stopped at the door. He grabbed Ivy's arm. "No. No, I cannot do this. We cannot enter a stranger's home."

"Dude, chill. Where's your sense of adventure?"

"I will not chill, Ivy. Where's your sense of reason?"

Dear Reader, Linus was right to be suspicious. Never go inside a stranger's house. Especially a witch. Haven't you read "Hansel & Gretel"? Nothing ends well with witches. Well, unless they're good witches, in which case, a witch's house can be a warm and welcoming place, which is nice.

"Fine. You can wait out here," Ivy said, stepping inside. "By yourself."

Linus looked about the yard. All of the doll heads turned at once in his direction and hissed. Though he instantly forgot, the chill it sent up his spine was enough to usher him through the front door.

The living room could have belonged to any grandmother, with its tweed couch, quilted blankets, potted plants, 1950s wood-box TV, and assortment of framed photos of smiling pets and people.

The kitchen was a different matter entirely. Shelves of all sizes lined the walls, each stacked with crystals, gemstones, athames, metal tins of dried herbs, glass jars full of insect and small mammal corpses. A tarantula crawled freely across several books toward a round aquarium of murky green slime with newts swimming in it.

Oracle snapped her fingers and a flame ignited on the stove. The lemur bounced across two counters, grabbed a kettle from a wall hook, filled it with water in the sink, then placed it over the open fire. Oracle moved the minute hand forward on a nearby clock, by four minutes. The kettle whistled. "Perfect timin'. Who wants some tea?" she asked, waving the kids to sit at the dining room table.

The lemur bounced about the kitchen, gathering chipped porcelain teacups, saucers, and spoons. The ring-tailed creature lifted the kettle, poured the steaming pink water into each cup, then used its petite fingers to place little cookies on each saucer. Carefully, the lemur passed them out to each guest. At some point when no one was watching, he'd put on a bow tie and a small top hat.

"Thank you, Gumbo," Oracle said to the lemur. She nodded to the others. "Drink up, but blow first. It's scalding."

"I am not drinking this," Linus whispered, pushing his teacup away. The lemur jumped up and down on the table, shrieking.

"Linus, don't be *rude*," Ivy said.

"Ivy, don't be *imbecilic*. What would Dad say if he knew we were accepting strange drinks from strange strangers claiming to be sorceresses?"

"I guess we'll never know since we're *not* telling him," Ivy growled.

Darling Reader, once again I must agree with Linus. *Never* accept a strange drink from a stranger. In it could be poison, or worse—licorice! Such a repugnant flavor. But seriously, do not accept food or drink from a person you do not know. I'd go so far as to advise not accepting food or drink from anyone, including people you *do* know. I was once poisoned by a person I thought to be my friend. It turns out she only wanted to kidnap me, steal me across the Atlantic, and make me fight a monster. Another bit of advice? Friends can be monsters, and monsters are... well, monstrous.

"I certainly am strange!" Oracle laughed. "But that ain't a strange drink. It's Razzle-dazzle Tea."

As if to spite her brother, Ivy took a sip. Her cheeks blushed instantly. "It tastes like blueberries. No wait... blueberry muffins...fresh out of the oven...just buttered!"

Curious, Will took a sip of his own. His cheeks flushed too. "Mine tastes like lemon-raspberry tart, from my favorite bakery in Brooklyn."

Oracle smiled. "Razzle-dazzle is a plant I grew myself. Tastes like whatever sweet ya love most. Tastes like dark chocolate and peppermint pretzels for me."

Linus pushed his teacup farther away. "Smells like danger to me."

Oracle Jones nodded to Linus's teacup. Will, Ivy, and

Linus leaned forward. The cup of tea—the tea he didn't drink—was empty, except for the wet remains and debris of a few pink tea leaves. They had settled around the cup in a bizarre pattern.

Linus shrugged. "I've seen stage magicians do it better."

"Do you know what tasseomancy is? Reading the patterns of tea leaves. Don't matter if ya drank or not. The cup was served and ya touched it. Your fate is written there now." Oracle picked up his cup and studied it. A grin crawled across her face and she giggled. "Ain't that a hoot?"

Oracle showed him the leaves. "*This* is a church roof, which you'll be under soon enough. *This* is a full moon, which you'll howl at. And *this* is a book that you will…well! Ain't that uncanny, and in-ter-estin'! I did not see you and magic gettin' along…"

"What?" Linus asked.

Oracle smirked. "You'll see."

Linus shook his head. "A prophecy with vague detail. How convenient. But you are incorrect. I do not attend church, I do not howl at celestial objects, and I am a man of science, not magic."

"If you say so." The witch laughed. "Now, I done gave ya drink and hospitality, as old custom demands. Manners are done, time for business. Y'all three are searchin' for answers, answers for missin' animals."

"How did you—" Ivy started.

Oracle raised a hand. "Don't interrupt, child. Listen and listen well. Fate and a fox brought y'all to my door. I'm obligated to help her, but a...another friend of mine made me promise to give ya a chance to get off this train before it leaves the station. What y'all are looking for is dangerous, and y'all risk everything by chasing it.

"Right now? This is your last chance to stop. Go home, forget what you've seen, and try to live normal lives."

"And Fitz?" Will asked.

"I'm afraid your dog is already mixed up in the dark business. Ya need to let him go if ya don't want to get involved. It may hurt now, but his life may save yours. It ain't fair, but sacrifices always gotta be made in the game of living."

"No way," Will said, "I don't accept that."

"Heed my warning, child. All three of ya'll be diggin' into matters far beyond your know. Ya keep marching forward to find them missin' pets, and you'll be stumbling down a rabbit hole into a larger labyrinth, one that'll take ya down a dangerous road. And the thing about road in life? Once ya start down some, there ain't no turnin' around. Y'all gotta keep truckin' forward, no matter what. Sometimes the only way through, is under."

Will asked, "Are you talking about the missing animals?"

Ivy added, "Or the monsters everywhere?"

Linus added, "How about the Vikings that vanished?"

"Everything is connected." The witch's tone turned even more serious. "Missing animals are the tip of a tree limb. You squirrels keep running up this branch looking for nuts, you'll see more and more of the Tree of Life—but you may not like what you learn. Your dog's life ain't the only thing in jeopardy—the fate of every soul in East Emerson is at stake."

Will thought of what the fox said. He repeated: "Save the animals, and save the town."

"Say all of it," the witch said.

Will pushed his memory. "Find the animals, destroy the crown. Save the animals, and save the town."

"There ya go," Oracle said. "But if y'all ain't up to it, walk away now."

"If we don't do this, what happens to East Emerson?" Will asked.

Gumbo leaped into Oracle's lap, shaking as if afraid. Oracle pet the lemur gently. She shook her head. "There are some things even I can't see."

"We're just kids," Will whispered. "What can we do?"

"Ya ain't giving yourself enough credit. Children can do anything they put their mind, body, and spirit to. Anything."

Will looked at Ivy, who looked at Linus, who looked at Will.

"Y'all want a quiet, normal life? Turn around, walk out my door, and never look back. But if ya wanna live life honest, full of impossible things ya can't yet imagine exist, things that once ya know, ya can't ever *un*-know? And maybe save the world in the process? Then step up."

Ivy smiled. "I've said it before, I'll say it again—normal is overrated. Let's adventure."

"And you, child of science?" Oracle Jones asked Linus.

"I believe in science, in the real world, not the impossible. But I must admit, there is a great deal that science cannot yet explain. I want to learn all there is, however improbable it seems. Consider my interest piqued."

Everyone turned to Will.

Will hesitated.

He thought about his dad leaving. About Marcellus and Brooklyn being so far away. He thought about his mom not being able to pay her bills. About Fitz running away, or being stolen. He thought about his parents' split. About being forced to move to East Emerson. There was so much he didn't have a say in. So many things that happened to him, that he couldn't control. But this?

This was his choice. And his alone.

Still, he was surprised when he answered, "Fitz is my dog, my best friend. I'll do anything to get him back. If the town is in jeopardy, that means so is my mom. I have to protect her. I'm in."

Oracle Jones smiled. "True grit all around. Glad to see. This town needs champions for the dark days a'comin'. Now it has three. Even if you are a bit young in the tooth."

At that moment, Will, Ivy, and Linus experienced the same sense of dread, washing up from their toes to their heads, as if plunging into a chilling river and pulled under.

"What do you mean dark days are coming?" Will asked.

"Y'all're gonna see soon enough, kid. Don't rush it. Enjoy these last days of quiet while ya can."

Linus crossed his arms. "I will not repudiate your claims, but I am curious if you have any circumstantial evidence to authenticate them?"

Oracle nodded to her pet. Gumbo walked across the table on his hind legs and gave Linus a hug, followed by a little lemur kiss on the cheek.

Will cooed, "That is the cutest thing I've ever seen in my whole life."

"OMG, can Gumbo come home with us?" Ivy begged.

But Oracle ignored them. She focused only on Linus. "Well? How did that make ya feel?"

Linus blushed. "It was…very sweet."

"Is that a fact?" the witch asked.

"Well, no, it is a feeling," Linus said.

"And feelings are not facts," the witch said, repeating what Linus had advised Will earlier that week. "Yet *feelings* rule people's lives. Witches are in tune with the world, with the universe. We pay attention to feelings, ours and others', and the vibrations beneath our feet and in the air. Feelings aren't science, but they can tell you things if you listen to them…

"For example, you, Linus, ya rely on science and facts because they make ya feel in control. You're brilliant and full of great potential, yes, but ya steer it all in the direction of academics to prove your worth, as if ya can control how the rest of the world sees ya.

"And you, Ivy, you're stronger than ya know, but ya feel weak, ya feel vulnerable. So ya try to prove to the world that you're tough and don't care what other folks say. But like Linus, you do. Why else would ya risk your life to prove to this town that what ya see is real?

"And you, Will… Guillermo, ya have so little confidence in yourself. In Brooklyn, ya stayed near Marcellus because he was charming and laughed a lot and made ya feel special. So did your father. But now you're on your own, and scared ya no longer matter. That you're nobody. If only ya believed that you're the hero of your own life. You need to find that confidence, child, or the town will be lost…"

Oracle's words stunned Linus, Ivy, and Will into utter silence. The witch glanced up at the clock and stood up. "Look at the time. Y'all need to git. Now." She pulled the table away from them, and hustled them out of their chairs. "Come on. Out!"

"Seriously?" Ivy gasped.

The old woman grabbed a walking stick and smacked the backs of their legs. "Yes, seriously. My soap stories are about to come on TV. And I don't miss my stories for nothin'. Not even the end of the world."

"End of the world?!" Will swallowed.

"Git!" With a snap of Oracle's fingers, the front door opened on its own. Even though none of them were walking, their shoes dragged across the floor, as if pulled by an invisible magnet. The lemur vaulted past them to turn on the old black-and-white television set. Then it sprung onto the couch and waved goodbye.

"Wait!" Will cried, grabbing on to the doorframe. "I have so many questions. Why can I see stuff? Where is Fitz? Where are the other missing animals? What's your role in all this? And what do you know about the silver fox?"

"Y'all'll know soon enough." The witch took a seat next to her lemur.

The door tried to close itself on them, but Ivy elbowed her arm and leg in first, then shouted, "Wait! You said you were supposed to give us gifts!"

"Dagnabbit." Oracle groaned. "Memory ain't what it

used to be. Glad ya remembered. Gumbo Jones, get off your tail and fetch them stones for our friends!"

The lemur bounced into the room and then back. He held three necklaces of twine, on the end of each was a jagged black rock, held in place by thin metal wire. Gumbo handed one each to Will, Ivy, and Linus.

Oracle noted, "Wear those everywhere. Don't take 'em off for nothin'. Black tourmaline protects a mind from bein' changed without consent. Also helps groundin' against telepathy, spells, and creates a shield from harmful electromagnetic fields."

"What do you know about EM fields?" Linus asked.

Oracle swatted her walking stick against the wall above her head. Linus gawked at several framed diplomas. "Is that a PhD in physics from MIT?"

Oracle smiled. "You can call me *Dr.* Jones if ya prefer, Linus." Then with a wave of her hand, a gust of wind shoved all three friends out onto the porch and the door slammed shut.

Will raced to her window, and pounded on the glass. "At least tell us what we do next!"

"Nothing," Oracle Jones called. "Don't go lookin' for mystery. It's comin' to you. *In three night's time, at the witch-*

ing hour, answer the scratch. Now go on! And don't come back till the fox brings you—or I'll put a hex on y'all!"

Then, Gumbo shut the lacy white curtains.

"Hex?" Ivy dragged her brother off the porch. "Nope! Not crossing her."

"She has a *doctorate*?" Linus whispered, dumbfounded.

"I still have so many questions," Will said.

As the three friends left, they did so with hearts full of joy, excitement, confusion, and fear. Each was so distracted, that no one noticed Linus's gift slip from his pocket. The twine necklace with a black stone fell to the ground and was lost.

Poor Linus. If only he had known…

Beloved Reader, one last piece of advice: while it is not smart to enter a strange witch's home or drink a strange witch's tea, it *is* smart to hold on to a strange witch's gift—as long as it's not a cursed talisman, which is hard to tell from a blessed talisman. My point being, yes, it is certainly difficult to determine which witches are well-meaning and which want to turn you into a roast dinner, *but* if a witch offers you a tourmaline necklace or some other form of protection, consider it a best practice to wear it.

You see, when Linus lost his necklace, he didn't know what a terrible mistake he'd made. But now *you* know. And as they say, knowing is half the battle.

And if you're wondering…yes, a battle is coming.

Chapter 9

monsters after midnight

✷

Will finished reading another *MonsterWorld* comic and tossed it onto the nightstand with the others. He looked at the clock. It still wasn't midnight. He kicked his bed, filled with anxiety. It had been days of agonizing waiting and Will was beyond frustrated. He wanted to know where Fitz was, if Fitz was okay, if the town was really in danger. He wanted answers to all of the questions Oracle Jones had left unanswered. He wanted to know how their adventure was going to come to them. Sitting around doing nothing was excruciating. So he paced the room for the next half hour.

The walkie-talkie on his nightstand lit up as Ivy's voice came through: *"Eyhay erdnay urdtay. Ouyay illstay awakeway?"*

Will snatched the borrowed two-way radio, pressed

the button, and said, "You know I don't understand Pig Latin, right?" He walked to his window and peered across the street.

Ivy waved from her own bedroom window, talking into the other walkie-talkie. "You should learn. Comes in handy all the time with me and Linus. Especially when Dad is trying to be all cool about us being adopted. He tries to celebrate Korean holidays or makes a big deal about Black History Month. *Osay annoyingway.*"

Will winced at the mention of a father. "I think that's really nice of him."

"It is. Don't get me wrong. I love my parents. But sometimes they try too hard."

"I know the feeling," Will admitted. He thought of his own mom, working another late shift at the hospital. "Thanks for letting me borrow the walkie-talkie."

"How else were we gonna chat until midnight? We can't exactly tell our parents we need cell phones so we can stay up late on monster watch."

"Where's Linus?" Will asked.

Ivy snorted. "He said, and I quote, 'Apologies, but mid-night is too late for a school night. Genius requires eight hours of an inactive nervous system, relaxed muscle posture, and a mostly suspended consciousness.' I think he was talking about sleep. Guess it's up to you and me."

"Are you stressed? I'm stressed. I mean, how are kids supposed to save a whole town?" Will asked. "Especially when we don't even know what we're saving it from?"

"Don't know, but I'm stoked to find out," Ivy admitted. "What time is it?"

"It's 11:57," Will answered. "Three minutes."

"The witching hour is midnight, right? What do you think Oracle thinks is going to happen? What do you think is going to happen? Are you as excited as I am?"

"*Excited* isn't the word I'd use," Will said. "I mean, since I've been in this town, I've seen werewolves, witches, wendigos, wargs, wraiths, wekufes, a wani, a waldgeist, a wanyūdō, and an Abenaki Wa-won-dee-a-megw."

"A wonder-what?" Ivy asked.

"Wa-won-dee-a-megw—it's a snail spirit that lives in trees. Apparently his horns are magic."

"How do you know all that?" Ivy noted.

"Some I found after researching online. Others I recognized from comics and video games and scary movies. Turns out a lot of the media monsters are based on real-life folklore. I keep waiting for Magneto to show up."

"What's a Magneto?"

"He's a mutant from the *X-Men* comics."

"Oh! Did I tell you who I saw today? An invisible man! Well, technically, I *didn't* see him. I saw his khakis, polo, and hat. He was hanging around outside the bank. I bet he's gonna rob it. What would you do if you were invisible?"

"Trade my powers to get new powers that'd help me find Fitz."

"Your pup means a lot to you, doesn't he?" Ivy asked.

"You have no idea," Will answered. He picked up a framed photo of him and Fitz as a puppy. "He's been part of our family for years. Or… I guess…our old family. We used to be so happy, Fitz, me, Mom, and Dad. Then him and Mom started fighting, about every little thing. It got real bad, screaming and stuff. Then last year, both of them turned into ghosts. Not real ghosts, but like, they never smiled, never laughed anymore. It felt like it was just me and Fitz. Then Dad left…they got a…a divorce…"

"You okay?" Ivy asked.

"Yeah," Will said. "That's the first time I've said it. *Divorce*. Guess I didn't want it to be true, like saying it would make it real. I think part of me hoped that moving to East Emerson was temporary. That Dad would show up to bring us home, or try to work things out with Mom—which is ridiculous. They haven't spoken in months.

"One day, my dad was just done, with my mom, with me... He was just gone. It's the most horrible thing that's ever happened to me. I know that's silly, but it felt like... like when he left, part of me...died. If it wasn't for Fitz, I don't think I would have been able to get out of bed. My whole life was falling apart, but every morning, Fitz woke me up, licked my face, and brought me his leash. Like he was reminding me that bad things happen, but I still have to get out of bed and walk him and get on with my life."

"That's really cool that you have Fitz," Ivy said. "I'm kinda jealous. A lot jealous actually. I've never had a best friend like that. I mean, I had a few friends until I started wearing my ring. Then they all thought I was a liar or a devil worshipper or just flat-out bonkers."

"You have Linus though," Will said.

"I do, yeah. And he's pretty okay, as brothers go. I mean, I love him. But we're so different, and he thinks I'm always playing pranks on him, but really it's the Flelfs. Or maybe Flelf is plural, I'm not sure. But they're like little people? Like, twelve-inches-tall little. Elves, but fluffier. They love playing tricks. Have you seen them in your house?

If not, you will. Some houses have problems with ants or cockroaches, ours has Flelfs. Anyway, I hope we find Fitz. Friends are good to have…" Ivy's voice trailed off, distant.

"You know, you're not alone anymore," Will said. "I see what you see. And it's fun hanging out with you. I'd say we're friends. Right?"

Will stared out across his lawn, past the street, into Ivy's window, where she was looking back. A smile appeared on her face. "Maybe. If you're lucky."

Will remembered the time. His heart dropped as he looked at the clock. "It's 12:04. Midnight came and went. Nothing happened."

"Maybe witch time is slow?" Ivy suggested.

"Or maybe Linus was right. Maybe Oracle Jones is just a faker—"

"Will," Ivy whispered, "very slowly go to your window."

At his window, Will saw only a clear sky full of stars and the moon. "To the west," Ivy added. A huge black swarm filled the sky, slowly blotting out the twinkling lights.

"Ivy, lock your window," Will commanded. "That's the same swarm that chased me at the fairgrounds."

Ivy pulled out a set of binoculars. "They're not bugs.

Too big. Birds and bats definitely, but I see other shapes too..."

"Maybe they're like Franken-Hare? Animals stitched together and all given wings," Will suggested.

Ivy strained to see. "That's weird."

"What?"

"I think... I think I see a cow. It doesn't have wings—but it's flying. A flying cow!" Ivy stifled a laugh. "Wait. The creatures are parting ways, flying in different directions all over town. I think... I see a few heading this way. Oh, no. Will. Brace yourself, I think I see—"

Fitz appeared outside Will's window, floating there. Will stumbled backward, knocking over his lamp, shattering the light bulb. Will grabbed his mouth so he wouldn't scream. He sat in the dark, staring as his dog pawed at the window.

"'Answer the scratch,'" Will repeated Oracle Jones's words. Will stood slowly.

Ivy's voice cried over the walkie-talkie "Will? Don't do it. Don't open your window."

"It's Fitz," Will said.

Fitz *hovered* outside his window, twenty feet above the ground. His dog whined, then licked the window.

Dear Reader, you might think this a joyful reunion. And on one hand, it was. Will was certainly happy to see his dog. However, he was *not* happy to see his dog *flying*. Nor was he happy to see that his dog's eyes were *glowing red*, or that Fitz now had sharp *vampire fangs* hanging down on either side of his panting tongue. You see, when you lose something, you hope desperately to get it back in the same condition. Unfortunately, this rarely (if ever) happens. I know from experience—once I loaned my *New Mutants* comic books to a friend, who I believed would treat them with respect. Instead, he spilled spicy salsa on them. Comic books are already thin pieces of paper, and to have them warped with wetness, then dried with stains from tomatoes and cilantro? Well, it's just not the same reading experience. The worst part? He didn't even apologize. Or share his chips and salsa! So rude.

What's that? Oh, yes, on with the story.

"Fitz? You okay, boy?" Will asked.

"Will! Will?!" Ivy shouted through the walkie-talkies.

Will's dog pawed at the second-story window again, the same way he did at the bathroom door when Will was taking too long. He wanted to be let in. Fitz barked, then whined, begging for Will to let him in. Will's hand hesitated at the lock. Fitz did a flip in the air, then panted, lowering his head, as if asking for an ear rub. Then he flew down to the yard and back, returning with a stick in his mouth. He wanted to play fetch.

Will spoke softly into the radio, "His eyes are red, he has fangs, and yeah, he's flying, but it's Fitz all right."

"Do *not* open your window!" Ivy said. "That's *not* your dog anymore—he's a vampire!"

"It's okay," Will said. "Fitz would never hurt me—would you, boy?"

Fitz barked a happy bark.

Will unlocked his window.

Ivy shouted, but Will didn't listen. He put down the walkie-talkie and opened the window. But Fitz didn't come inside.

"Why isn't he coming in?" Then Will recalled: vampires have to be *invited* inside.

Ivy saw what was happening and shouted into the radio, "Don't do it, don't invite him—"

"Come inside, Fitz," Will said.

This, Fearful Reader, was a foolish thing to do. When you are staring a vampire in the face—whether it's a vampire pet or a vampire friend or a vampire parent—and your friend is warning you *not* to invite it in, you should listen to said friend. It is both logical and reasonable to *not* invite a vampire inside your home. Vampires like blood, and if a vampire is trying to get inside your house, they probably want *your* blood. But Will—as with so many foolish people—decided to listen to his heart instead of his head. Such a silly *human* thing to do.

Ivy pulled her own hair as she watched from across the street. Fitz leaped through the window and tackled Will. Over the walkie-talkie, she heard yelps and shrieks and slobbering sounds.

"Oh, god, Fitz is devouring him," Ivy whispered to herself. "Will is puppy chow—or worse, vampire chow!"

The walkie-talkie squawked again with more cries and muffled sounds. Ivy shuddered. "Oh, no. Does that mean Will's a vampire? Do I have to cut his head off? Is that even how you destroy a vampire? Or do I just tie Will up outside and wait for the sun to come up?"

"I'm fine," Will laughed through his radio. "Fitz is just happy to see me. He won't stop licking me. It tickles!"

"He's gonna eat you!" Ivy said.

"Don't be ridiculous," Will said. "Meet me outside."

When Ivy finally came out, she wore her full hockey

uniform: pads, mask, gloves, and stick. Fitz was in his harness, held by his leash, only Will wasn't walking him. He anchored Fitz who flew in circles overhead. "It's so much more fun to watch him chase his tail in the air."

"Looks like you're not the only one with a missing pet that's turned up," Ivy noted. Up and down the street, vampire pets were scratching at the windows and doors of their owners. "I recognize some of those from the fliers at school—Jenny Tanaka's missing ferret, Digby Bronson's missing boa constrictor, and that's Gertrude York's missing—"

"Don't say it!" Will started.

But too late, Ivy finished "—cat."

Fitz's ears perked up at the word. He sniffed the air, spotted his prey, then took off like a bullet, flying after the fat orange cat, dragging Will behind him. "*Whooa, boy!*"

"Let go!" Ivy shouted.

"No! I'm not losing my dog again!"

Even as his feet lifted off the ground, Will refused to let go of the leash. Sure, Fitz could fly, but he wouldn't get far with Will weighing him down. Or so Will thought. When the York cat went up, so did Fitz—pulling Will behind him. A few inches, then a few feet, then—

Ivy jumped, wrapping her arms around Will's waist. That didn't stop Fitz either. The vampire canine floated higher and higher into the air as he followed the cat. Five feet, ten feet, twenty feet—

"How strong is Fitz?!" Ivy cried.

"Not this strong!" Will answered, clinging to the leash. "Watch out!"

Will and Ivy swung left to avoid slamming into a lamppost. The lights lined the street, and Fitz was flying right toward them as the cat swerved between them. Ivy and Will swung back and forth, lifting their legs or arching their bodies to dodge each one.

"Trees!" Ivy shouted. The pair tried not to scream as Fitz dragged them through the top of a tree. And then another.

Will spit out a mouthful of leaves. "Fitz! Down, boy!" But his dog was too focused on the cat.

"He's not listening," Will groaned.

Ivy looked down as the ground got farther away. "Well, whatever you do, don't let go."

Fitz chased the cat left, right, up, down, and backward, attracting the attention of other vampire animals. Several dogs joined the chase, as did a raccoon, several pigeons, some rats… Once again, a shadowy swarm of vampire animals were chasing Will. He hoped they just wanted to play—and weren't hungry.

"The cat's flying toward the city center," Ivy said, still desperately clinging to Will's waist. "If we can get Fitz low enough, we can try to swing around the lamppost or the gazebo, like a tetherball. We'll use our weight, and the leash, to anchor him."

"Good plan," Will said.

"REEEOOWWWWRR!" The York cat hissed and dove down. Fitz followed, straight under the roof of the gazebo. Will and Ivy threw their bodies to the right, swinging around the solid wooden post. They circled the post, slammed into the base, then braced themselves. Fitz dragged the leash up the sharp edge. The leash snapped.

"Fitz! Come back!" Will shouted. But his dog took off after the cat.

"Will, we have other problems," Ivy whispered.

Dozens of animals swarmed overhead, spinning in a giant spiral, chasing one another: chickens chasing dogs chasing cats chasing parrots chasing ferrets chasing pigs chasing gerbils chasing hamsters chasing snakes chasing goldfish chasing cows chasing chickens. There was even a horse flying among the terrifying tornado of vampires.

"Is every pet in this town a bloodsucker?" Will asked.

"They didn't used to be," Ivy answered, "but this explains why pets have gone missing and why kids at school look so tired. Their pets keep them up at night, then the town curse makes them forget."

"Yeah, but *who* is turning them into vampires? And why?"

A ferret flew through the air like a ribbon, and dived toward the only part of Ivy that was left exposed by her hockey uniform: her neck. It nipped her. "Ow! It tried to bite me!"

Then a potbellied pig flew down at Will. He ducked. When he looked up, he saw the entire swarm had taken notice. "That's not good."

"No, it's not," Ivy said. "*Run!*"

Ivy and Will ran. More and more of the animals dived after them, like cats chasing mice, or like vampires chasing necks, or like vampire cats chasing human children's necks. Oh, wait, it wasn't *like* that, it *was* that. "Cover your neck!" Ivy shouted at Will as she swatted away a fanged

Chihuahua. "Bad dog! Bad! Suddenly I'm glad Dad is allergic to pet dander."

"The bathroom!" Will pointed. "Let's hide in there."

Ivy got their first. She yanked on the door. "It's locked!"

Will scanned the park. They had nowhere to hide.

"Is this really how my life ends?" Will asked. "Eaten by animals? Is this because I eat meat? If I survive this, I'm becoming a vegetarian. Well—except for pepperoni. I couldn't possibly give up pizza."

"Do you always talk this much in life-or-death situations?" Ivy asked. She was busy batting away squirrels and gerbils and mice with her gloves and her hockey stick. "Ha! Take that! And that! Hey, this is just like being a goalie. Except, you know, with rodents instead of pucks."

"Incoming dog!!" Will shouted.

A Great Dane flew at Ivy, mouth open. She raised her stick up just in time, managing to shove it into the dog's mouth like a horse bridle bit. The dog snapped, gnashing its teeth. "Ew. You got stink breath, dog."

With a loud crunch, it chomped straight through the hockey stick, breaking it in two. "Hey! It took me six months to save up for that!" Full of fury, Ivy used her rage to kick the dog up and into the air.

Now, Dear Reader, I *never* condone cruelty toward animals. I believe all creatures, big and small, have as much right to life, liberty, and the pursuit of happiness as humans. Even though birds often peck at my eyes, and cats always hiss at me, I love them as deeply as I love my pet dog, Toby, a terrier, who loves me despite being a monster. I myself am even a *strict* vegetarian...well, excepting fish, as I do love my sushi. My point being, children should *never* hit or kick or hurt animals...

Unless of course, those animals have turned into vampires and are trying to devour you and it is your life or theirs. I suppose that's an exceptional exception to the rule.

The Great Dane only flew so far before it course-corrected. As it flew back, the dog was joined by an Anatolian shepherd, an English mastiff, two ostriches, a llama, and a beautiful black horse. All of the red-eyed, fanged animals hissed and dived toward Ivy and Will.

"Sorry I dragged you into this," Will said.

"Are you kidding?" Ivy smirked. "This is the most fun I've had in ages."

They both crouched down, covering their heads, waiting to be devoured. But at the last possible moment, Fitz flew in front of them and stopped. He barked a terrifying monstrous roar at the oncoming beasts.

As they barked and hissed and neighed back, Fitz stood his ground. The mastiff tried to get past, but Fitz bit his neck, and the mastiff retreated with a whimper.

"*GRRRRRR...*" Fitz growled. He wouldn't let anything come near Will or Ivy. He guarded them as protectively as a momma bear would her cubs. He bared his teeth viciously, warning the other animals not to come any closer.

The other vampiric animals backed away, slowly returning to the sky.

When it was safe, Will threw his arms around Fitz's neck. "You saved us, boy! I knew you weren't a bad vampire. Good dog!"

Fitz licked Will's face.

Somewhere in the distance, a low whistle blew. As if a dinner bell sounded, all of the animals turned their heads in unison, looking to the north. Together, they swirled up and flew in the direction of the piercing sound.

Fitz's eyes turned sad, licked Will's face again, then floated up to join the others.

"Wait, Fitz!" Will cried. "Don't you wanna come home?"

His dog gazed down at him, then looked after the

other animals, conflicted. Fitz whined, hesitating. The whistle sounded again.

Fitz gave one last sad look to Will, then ascended into the sky to catch up with the other vampire animals.

"Fitz, come back!" Will cried. But his dog either didn't hear, or didn't listen. And just like that, Will lost his best friend for a second time. Somehow, this time, it hurt much more.

Chapter 10

questions and answers

✷

Ivy dropped her lunch tray on the cafeteria table with a loud *clack!* Some of her mashed potatoes splashed onto Will's hand. "I can't believe we have to go to school when the whole town is in danger. Oracle Jones should've given us a magic necklace that gets us out of class."

"Perhaps you should go to the principal's office and explain our dire situation," Linus noted. He pulled the plastic lid from his lunch box revealing fragrant beef bulgogi, rice, kimchi, and a chocolate chip cookie.

"You think that would work?" Ivy asked.

"No," Linus said. "I do not."

"Boo," Ivy said, slumping into her seat. "Wanna trade lunches?"

"Absolutely not," Linus said. "This is the last of the kimchi batch we made two weeks ago. And Dad's bulgogi is even better the day after. You're the one who declined this morning's selection."

"I thought it was pizza and fries day!" Ivy shoved her fingers into her mashed potatoes with a groan. "My life is a fart."

Will would have laughed, but since Fitz had vanished a second time, he couldn't seem to muster any happiness. Will added, "My life is a fart too."

"Your lives are *not* anal gas," Linus stated. "If what you told me about the other night is true, you should be grateful to be alive."

"It happened," Will said. "Trust us."

"Trust is difficult for a man of science," Linus whispered.

"Okay, so we're back to square one," Ivy said. "How's the fox's clue go again?"

"Find the animals, destroy the crown. Save the animals, and save the town."

"What crown?" Ivy asked.

Will stirred his mashed potatoes. "No idea."

"Then how do we find the animals?" Ivy asked.

The three sat there, staring at each other. No one had any answers.

Linus pulled a pencil from his pocket protector and tapped it against his forehead. “Perhaps we’re approaching this wrong. If we apply the scientific method, step one is ask the question, Where are the animals? Step two is research, as in gathering information through observation.”

“You’re taking the fun out of this by making it sound like homework,” Ivy said.

“No, keep going,” Will said.

Linus waved his hand to the quiet cafeteria. “Observe—Danny Patel and the other football players are half-asleep at their table. Melissa Hobbs and her cheerleader squad also look tired, in addition to being pale. Kendra Washington and the other band kids also appear out of sorts. Usually the cafeteria is abuzz with chatter, laughter, and the occasional drama. But there is very little now.”

Linus continued, “Usually I would consider a logical explanation—perhaps the stress of academia and/or extracurricular activity is too much for our peers. But given our secret knowledge—though I am still cautious to believe—might suggest something else. Your hypothesis is that vampiric pets are visiting our classmates at night, keeping them awake, and possibly feeding from them. Of course, if this town is 'cursed' as Oracle suggested, then their minds would immediately forget the experience—their physical bodies, however, would not."

"Where is this going?" Ivy asked.

"I suggest we look for a common link between the owners of missing pets."

"Linus, you're a genius," Will said.

Linus smiled. "I often think so."

In fourth period French, Ivy leaned forward and tapped Jenny Tanaka on the shoulder. "Hey, Jenny, long time no chat. How's your pet? You have a ferret, right? What's his story?"

Jenny began to cry. "Captain Fluffcoat's been gone for over a month. I miss him so much."

"Captain Fluffcoat?" Ivy snorted. She tried not to laugh. "When's the last time you saw him?"

"Before he went missing! Duh!" Jenny snapped.

"Right. Sure. But, like, maybe you dreamed about him last night? Saw him flying outside your window? Maybe he was a vampire?"

"Why are you asking such stupid—" Jenny started... then something clicked. "Actually, I have been dreaming about him lately. And he's always flying. How'd you know that?"

Ivy shrugged. "Just a wild guess. Anything else you can tell me? Like, what kinda music does he listen to? You walk your ferret? What's he eat?"

"You are so weird," Jenny whispered. "He doesn't listen to music, he's a ferret. You don't walk ferrets like dogs. And he eats a special food Dr. Pamiver prescribed for him."

"Arrête de murmurer en classe, étudiants!" Ms. Rosseau shouted. "Ou je vais te donner à manger aux dinosaures."

Ivy smirked. "Vraiment? J'aimera bien donc être mangè par un Tyrannosaurus rex."

Ms. Rousseau smiled. "Une merveilleuse façon de mourir. Et votre francais est super, Ivy."

"Merci beaucoup," Ivy replied.

In fifth period advanced calculus, Linus politely waited until the teacher was at the board to lean forward and whisper to Gertrude York. "It has come to my attention your cat is missing."

Gertrude turned in her chair. "Have you seen Kitty Katastrophe?"

"No. But a friend of mine has lost his dog and—"

"Dogs are dumb. I'm a cat-person," Gertrude said.

"Yes, well, be that as it may, if you have any information that might—"

Gertrude pulled a full-color flier from her backpack, and handed it to Linus. "Kitty's coat is a majestic orange sherbet, he has a little white tuft on his right paw, and weighs twenty-two pounds. Dr. Pamiver says he's overweight, but I think fat-shaming is rude, even for a doctor. Kitty's been missing for three weeks. If you see him anywhere, Mom and Dad are offering a cash reward of a hundred dollars."

"Good to know," Linus said. He braced himself to ask his next and likely final question.

You see, Anxious Reader, like myself, Linus is not great at public speaking, or speaking to people at all. Certainly, we could give a keynote to a large grouping of trees. But conversing with actual humans, face-to-face, is rather a different challenge. When speaking to others, especially when asking odd questions to other students, Linus felt a great deal of anxiety. If you have nerves of jelly, like Linus and myself, you understand. If you do not, consider yourself lucky. I will do my best *not* to envy you so much that I wish you trip and fall and embarrass yourself next time you are in public. Anyhow…

Linus took a deep breath. He closed his eyes, and asked, "I know this sounds ridiculous, but is there any chance your animal companion has become a vampire and returns to your bedroom window each night to keep you awake and possibly feed upon your blood?"

Gertrude raised her hand, and shouted, "Mr. Villalobos! Linus is whispering horrible things to me!"

The hirsute math teacher raised an eyebrow, pointing his ruler at Linus. "Mr. Cross. I'm disappointed. Up until now, I thought you were a model student. Please do *not* bother your peers. This is advanced calculus—*not* a place for you to flirt."

As the other kids snickered, Linus shrank backward into his seat. Linus had never been reprimanded by a teacher before. He wondered if this would affect his grades or if this would be put on his permanent record, or if it would prevent him from getting into a good college…

Luckily, before his worries could spiral too far, he noticed Gertrude's neck. It had two tiny scabs—perfect cat-sized fang puncture marks.

In sixth period science, Mr. Zhang announced, "Everyone find a lab partner." Reluctantly, Will forced himself to sit down next to football player Digby Bronson.

"What do you think you're doing?"

Will took a deep breath, reminding himself this was for Fitz. "I couldn't help but notice you're looking really pale. And yawning a lot. Like you're not sleeping. And, uh…that you lost your snake."

Digby glared at Will. "I didn't lose him. Someone stole him."

"Right, right. Of course. Um…"

"What're you getting at? You know something about Billy Snakespeare?"

"No! I don't know anything," Will said. "My dog's missing. So are a bunch of pets. I hoped you, maybe, like, knew something… I mean, have you seen anything? Maybe late at night…?"

Digby's scowl softened. "Nah. But I dream about him sometimes. Flying around outside, banging his tail on the window, doing his lil' snake tongue thing. Then he drinks my blood. But last night, I dreamed about being naked at school. That's the worst, everyone staring at me and I can't find my tighty-whities and—" Digby caught himself. "Don't tell anyone that part, or I'll snap your spine like a twig, got it?"

"I won't. Promise," Will said. "Um… I hope you get your snake back."

Looking away, Digby said, "Thanks. I hope you get your dog back too. If you haven't, maybe put up a flier at the vet's. Dr. Pamiver's a good guy. He treats my snake. And most pets in town too."

Will sighed. He was never going to figure this out.

The bell rang. Somehow Will was always late to gym class. He could swear that the school hallways changed colors and directions on him every day, just to confuse him. He quickly changed into his PE uniform, then ran into the gymnasium. The whole class was already lying down doing sit-ups.

The gym teacher, Coach Ewflower, blew her whistle at Will. "Tardy again, new kid. Drop and gimme twenty."

Will dropped and did twenty push-ups. Well, technically, he did eleven and a half. After that, he struggled to get higher than an inch.

Coach Ewflower rolled her eyes. "Just join the others."

Will lay down between Ivy and Linus. "Is she ever nice?"

"No," Linus whispered.

"She loves me," Ivy said. "Probably because I win at every sport we play. Everyone loves winners."

"Not sore winners," Linus added.

Will asked, "Either of you have any luck with questions?"

Ivy shook her head. Linus noted, "Gertrude York has fang marks on her neck."

The whistle sounded again. The coach shouted at them, "Hunter! Cross! Other Cross! Less talking, more working out. We're going to a hundred today, class! Then a hundred jumping jacks, a hundred lunges, and a hundred push-ups. Then jogging. I hear any complaints, we'll do two hundred."

Will, Ivy, and Linus sat up, lay back, sat up, lay back, sat up, lay back. "Maybe she's the villain," Will whispered.

"That is a rather epic leap in logic," Linus said. "If she is our culprit, what is her motive?"

"I was kidding," Will whispered. He noticed the coach trying to motivate a sleeping student on the other side of the gymnasium. "I don't think having a bunch of tired, bloodless students makes her job any easier."

The coach blew her whistle. "Jumping jacks!"

Our trio hopped up and began jumping and throwing their arms over their heads. Will and Linus looked like they might pass out. Ivy wasn't even sweating as she exercised and considered their mystery.

"My brain is all hurty from all this thinking. Come through, little brother," Ivy said. "You're the brains of our operation."

"Can you not see I am trying?" Linus wheezed. "It is hard to think while all the blood flows to my muscles."

"What muscles?" Ivy asked with a wink.

"Har-har," Linus growled. "You realize I got in trouble

today. I've never been reprimanded by a teacher before. I did *not* enjoy the feeling."

"Aww, I'm so proud of you, little brother," Ivy said. "Don't worry. It gets easier each time."

"I do not want it to get easier," Linus said. "I want my teachers to like me."

The coach blew her whistle. "Lunges!"

"The whistle," Ivy whispered, as she lunged, her hands on her hips. "Will, remember? The other night, a whistle sounded and all the animals returned. Maybe it really is Coach."

Linus shook his head. "Unlikely. Owning a whistle hardly proves guilt. I own a whistle."

"And Dr. Pamiver's office is full of dog whistles," Will added.

The three friends stopped working out, staring at each other.

Ivy said, "Jenny Tanaka mentioned Dr. Pamiver."

"As did Gertrude York," Linus added.

"Dr. Pamiver treated Digby's snake. And I took Fitz to him for a checkup a few days before he disappeared. And that squirrel! He was close to dead and Dr. Pamiver fixed him with a single shot." Will felt a chill run up his spine. "It's him, isn't it?"

"It is logical," Linus said. "The primary common link between the animals would be the town vet. But it's his job to keep pets healthy and—"

"—immortal?" Ivy said. "Certainly would make his job easier."

"Yeah, but if all the animals were healthy forever, he wouldn't be able to make money," Will said. "So why do it?"

"Maybe he wants to sell pets that live forever," Ivy said.

"Interesting theory," Linus said. "Last year, I desperately wanted a set of lab mice until I read about their short life span. The thought of forming an emotional attachment and losing them was too much. Perhaps the vet is tired of seeing animals die."

"It doesn't matter what his motive is," Will said. "If it's true, we have to save Fitz and the rest of the animals."

"So what now?" Linus asked. "Tell our parents?"

"Tell them what?" Ivy asked. "'Oh, hey, uh, the vet is turning the town's pet population into his own personal bloodsucking army.' I don't think so. We're on our own."

“Okay, the fox said, ‘Find the animals,’” Will added. “Where would Dr. Pamiver keep them?”

“I suggest we start with the most obvious place,” Linus said, “at the vet clinic itself.”

“But how do we get in and snoop around?” Will asked.

Ivy smiled. “You realize what tomorrow night is, right? It’s Halloween.”

Linus rolled his eyes. “Ivy, we need to focus on the animals, not asking strangers for candy.”

Ivy rolled her eyes back doubly hard. “I know that. But tomorrow night, all of the local stores and businesses are staying open late for trick-or-treaters.”

“And?” Will asked.

“Find a costume,” Ivy said. “Tomorrow night, we’re getting dressed up. But instead of treats, we’re going in for tricks…”

Chapter 11

Halloween

✶

At 5:00 p.m., Will put on his costume, grabbed his bike, and met Ivy and Linus in the street between their houses. At the same time, all three friends asked one another the same question: "What are you supposed to be?"

"I'm a fencer," Ivy said.

"A fence?" Will asked.

"A fenc*er*. Someone who fences. Thus the fencing sword," Ivy explained. "I figured if there was the possibility of battling bloodsuckers, I should have my whole body covered up. And now it is."

"That is actually quite sensible," Linus said. "I wish I had thought of that."

"Too bad, so sad, but not mad about it," Ivy said with a wink. "Why are you dressed like an old man?"

"I am costumed as the most brilliant theoretical physicist of all time," Linus said. "Albert Einstein."

"That mask is super creepy," Will noted. "Masks creep me out almost as much as clowns."

"What are you?" Linus asked. "A wet paper towel?"

"A sad snowman?" Ivy asked.

"Dirty dry cleaning?"

"A used tissue?"

"I'm a ghost." Will's face was flushed with embarrassment under the white sheet. He didn't know how to explain that he was too poor to afford a store-bought costume. He'd had to make his own by cutting eye holes out of an old sheet.

Dear Reader, homemade costumes are nothing to be ashamed of. Money is often tight with many families, and as they say, "Necessity is the mother of invention." The proverb means, roughly, the primary driving force behind most inventions is need. I started life with very little, you see, and learned very quickly that if I needed something I would have to build it myself. Unfortunately, building a television is very difficult, so I had to entertain myself. Turns out, I am not as funny as I'd like. My comedy is as wretched as my face, and no one wants to see either. Anywho…

The trio got on their bikes and pedaled out of their neighborhood. As they passed a group of kids laughing and ringing doorbells, Ivy looked longingly. "Are you sure we shouldn't do a *little* trick-or-treating before our big shakedown? I mean, sugar will give us extra energy."

"Sugar will rot our teeth," Linus stated. "Or is this a sad attempt at bailing on the plan?"

"I'm not bailing!" Ivy shouted. A second later, she muttered, "Just maybe a little…nervous."

"Me too," Will said.

"Me to the third power," Linus added.

"It's probably good that we're all nervous," Will said. "It'd be dumb if we weren't. We're about to go face down a vampire nest and a mysterious big bad."

"When you put it like that, it sounds like a really *not*-good idea," Ivy muttered.

"Nonsense. We have a plan, and a plan is a strategy for success," Linus noted. "My backpack is stocked with all that we need."

"How long do we have until the sun goes down?" Will asked.

"The sun will vanish under the horizon at exactly 6:08 p.m.," Linus said. "I have an alarm set on my watch."

"With any luck, we'll get in, save the animals, destroy the crown—whatever that is—grab Fitz, and be home, safe and sound before bedtime," Will said. Linus and Ivy made doubtful faces. "What? It might…could…maybe happen."

The friends rode east. Trick-or-treaters were everywhere, dressed up in costumes, looking for candy. Just as Ivy had said, every business in central East Emerson was open for trick-or-treaters, including the veterinary clinic.

The trio hid their bikes behind the sign, then peeked inside the windows. Dr. Pamiver was there along with an assistant and the receptionist, handing out candy to kids. Ivy snorted, trying to stifle a laugh. "Are the vet people dressed up as the Three Little Pigs?"

"They are," Will answered. "Doesn't exactly scream *bad guy*, does it?"

"Focus," Linus whispered. He led them to the side parking lot and hid between two cars. He unloaded his backpack along with an itemized checklist. He handed out the items as he went down the list, placing a check next to each item:

- *Garlic Chains*
- *Silver Crosses*
- *Wooden Stakes*
- *Holy Water Guns*
- *Hand Ax*
- *Firecrackers*
- *Lighter*

"What about the black rock necklace Oracle gave us?" Ivy asked. "I'm wearing mine."

"Me too," Will said.

Linus gritted his teeth. "I lost mine. I am certain it will not be necessary. I came well prepared." He patted a large bulge in the fanny pack clipped around his waist.

"What's that?" Will asked.

"Something for emergencies."

"What's the ax for?" Ivy asked.

"My internet research revealed chopping off a vampire's head was an effective way to end its life," Linus stated.

"Yeesh, Linus," Ivy shouted, snatching the ax away, and shoving it into her belt. "We're not cutting off anyone's head. Take it down a notch, will you?"

"Apologies. I only wanted to be prepared for any eventuality."

"Wait a minute, are those *my* firecrackers?" Ivy growled.

"We need them, dear sister. For the good of our little supernatural society."

"The *Supernatural Society*? Is that what we're calling ourselves now?"

"It's shorter than *Monsters, Myth, Magic, & Mad Science Mystery Club*," Will said with a grin.

"We can discuss organization titles later," Linus said. "I just lit the fuse."

"What fuse?" Will asked.

Linus held up row after row after row of a long bunch of tied-together Black Cat firecrackers, attached to more firecrackers at the end. He tossed them as far as he could. "We should move."

BRAK-A-KRAK!

Linus led Ivy and Will around the back of the vet clinic

to the other side. When the vet staff and the trick-or-treaters rushed outside to the parking lot to investigate the explosions, the sleuthing trio ran inside, through the lobby, and into the back room.

"Whoa! Next time warn us!" Ivy hissed at her brother.

"I presumed an adventure like the one we are undertaking should best be entered like a cold swimming pool—by diving in without thinking."

"Guess that works," Will said. "Linus, you watch the Three Little Pigs. Let us know when they come back in. Ivy, with me."

Linus checked the window. The Three Little Pigs were trying to stamp out the firecrackers with their shoes. Kids were cheering while the adults looked confused. But as the Black Cats finished, the fuse led to the bigger fireworks. As they went off, colorful pinwheels exploded, shooting in every direction. Linus had used every single one of Ivy's hidden stash of firecrackers. He hoped it would keep the vet and the trick-or-treaters distracted long enough.

Meanwhile, Will and Ivy rushed through the office. They checked the closets, the operation rooms, and finally the overnight room. “Uh…where are the animals?” Ivy asked as she stared at all of the empty cages lining the walls.

“There’s not a single animal here,” Will said. He couldn’t believe this. Some part of him hoped this would be simple, that they would just run in, grab Fitz, release the other animals, and escape. “Fitz! Where are you boy?!”

“*Shhhh*,” Ivy hissed. “The vet’ll hear you. We have to grab Linus and leave. If we get caught—”

“What about the town?” Will said. “We have to save the animals.”

“I know, but, ” Ivy said, “what if we were wrong? What if Dr. Pamiver isn’t the bad guy?”

In anger, Will slammed his hands on the desk. A secret panel on the side fell open, and a small golden pyramid fell out with a scroll. Will grabbed both, but held up the triangular prism. It was golden on one side, with gibberish on the sides, but on the bottom, he noticed some kind of key code…

“Is that a paperweight?” Ivy asked.

“It’s the golden pyramid that Oracle told us about. We were right!”

Linus ran into the room and shut the door. "The Three Little Pigs stopped the firecrackers prematurely with a water hose. They'll be back in short order. We must escape."

"No!" Will cried. "Pamiver is the bad guy. We have to find Fitz."

"If he is the bad guy, we need to stay alive to find Fitz. Now, come on," Ivy said. She pulled Will after Linus. Reluctantly, he went, shoving the pyramid and scroll in his pocket.

The trio followed the signs pointing toward the back exit. They ran through a storage room toward the back doors. But only a few feet from freedom, Will stopped. "Wait!" He pointed at a wooden door in the floor, marked with giant letters:

VIII

"The cemetery well had a *V*. The hole Oracle Jones found us in had an *IV*. And the trapdoor in the Svengali Fairgrounds said *III*," Will noted.

"So?" Ivy asked.

"They are not letters, they are numbers," Linus answered. "They are Roman numerals."

"Numbers to all the entrances..." Will realized "...to the *tunnel system* underneath East Emerson."

"Tunnels?" Ivy whispered, "Oracle—she said sometimes the best way through is *under*."

"It is all coming together." Linus closed his eyes, thinking hard. "If the animals lived here, and there are tunnels running under Emerson, they could take the tunnels to fly out through the amusement park so as not to draw attention to Pamiver."

"Help me with this door," Will said. Together, the three friends lifted. The door fell backward, revealing a set of stone stairs, just like those below the Cave of Doom.

"Will, wait!" Ivy whispered. But too late. Will took Linus's flashlight and charged ahead into the darkness.

Linus pulled two glow sticks from his pack and handed one to his sister. They snapped and shook them. The neon sticks cast an eerie green glow over the siblings. Together, they took a deep breath, then followed their friend down into the tunnels.

"Will?" Ivy whispered. At the bottom of the staircase was another tunnel, like the one they'd been trapped in a week before. “I can’t see in this dang thing.” Ivy pulled off her fencing helmet.

“Same.” Linus pulled off his own mask. He adjusted his glasses, then surveyed the stone tunnel. He pulled a piece of chalk out of his pocket and drew a large arrow, pointing back to the stairs. “So we do not get lost.”

“Good thinking,” Ivy said.

“Why, sister, I do believe you just paid me a compliment. That might be a first.” Linus smiled.

Ivy smiled back. “Don’t get used to it.”

Linus and Ivy walked farther into the tunnel, holding their glow sticks up. The emerald glow barely pierced the darkness. A shadow jumped out in front of them and grabbed them. “Hey—”

Ivy and Linus both screamed, clinging to each other, before realizing it was only Will. “Don’t sneak up on us like that, you giant jerk!” Ivy shouted, punching Will in the arm as hard as she could.

“Ow!” Will rubbed his arm. “That hurt!”

“Good! Don’t run off! We’re a team, remember?!”

“Sorry,” Will said. “I thought of Fitz and couldn’t help it. But the tunnel splits here into three passageways. How are we going to find anything?”

"Read the signs?" Linus whispered. He guided Will's flashlight up to a giant message carved into the granite face:

← GSV XVNVGVIB

GSV DRGXS'H SLFHV →

GSRH DZB GL GSV HOVVKRMT TILFMWH ↑

"Another code without a cipher," Ivy said.

"Actually..." Will retrieved the golden pyramid from his pocket. He flipped it upside down and showed the others:

"It's a cipher wheel..." Ivy said. "I love secret messages." She started matching up the letters and spelling out the clue in her head.

A proud grin crossed Will's face. "Everything's falling into place. The pyramid, the codes. What's it say, Ivy?"

Ivy pointed. "The wall says, that way to the cemetery, that way to the witch's house, and...this way to the... sleeping grounds? That doesn't make sense."

"Unless you're a vampire," Will whispered. "Vampires would sleep underground during daytime. Come on!"

Will pulled the others down a short tunnel and into a giant cavern. The neon green glow of their glow sticks lit the floor—nothing. "No..." Will whispered. "There's nothing here..."

"Uh, Will," Ivy whispered, "look up."

At first, Will thought the ceiling was moving. Then he realized: it was blanketed by animals, sleeping in a giant animal cuddle puddle as if gravity had reversed itself. Horses, cows, pigs, dogs, cats, gerbils, ferrets, birds, even snakes—were all sleeping together like best friends at a sleepover.

"I know this should be a cute calendar in the making, but I'm totally freaking out," Ivy whispered.

“I don’t see anything,” Linus whispered in frustration.

Ivy clamped her hand over her brother’s mouth. She pointed up, then made fangs with his fingers, silently noting that they were in a nest of vampires. She raised a finger over her lips. Will noticed that for the first time, Linus had to completely trust Ivy. But rather than argue, Linus went quiet.

Will flashed his light over the ceiling slowly, searching for his dog. And there he was, curled up at the edge of the pile spooning a dozen small kittens. Moving his lips without a sound, Will asked the others, *How do we get him down?*

They both shrugged.

Suddenly, Linus’s watch went off. *BEEP-BEEP-BEEP-BEEP!*

“Shut it off!” Ivy hissed.

“It’s my alarm,” Linus whispered, “timed for when the sun sets…which means—”

All of the animals above began to stir. Red eyes blinked awake, fanged-mouths yawned. Some animals began to stretch. Others stood upside down on the ceiling and shook off their sleep. Some simply stared down at the trio who had invaded their home. In a massive torrential downpour of feathers, fur, fins, scales, and udders, the animals swarmed down around the friends, blocking them from going anywhere. They were surrounded on every side.

Fitz recognized Will and swooped in. But even his barks and snarls didn't sway the hungry animals. And Will knew his dog couldn't defend them against an army.

Ivy pushed Linus behind her, protectively. "Will…what do we do?!"

"I don't know," Will said, pressing his shoulder to Ivy's. He flashed his light back and forth, trying to keep the animals at bay.

"Maybe you should ask me," a voice said from behind them. An eerie crimson illumination flooded the room, overpowering the darkness. The animals backed away, as if scared.

The trio turned to see Dr. Pamiver standing behind them. The short, round man wore a gleaming crimson crown on his shiny balding head. He glared at the three kids with scarlet eyes, his hands curling into fists. The edges of his lips curled into a sinister grin, revealing two piercing-white vampire fangs. "It seems you know my secret. I guess the real question now is—*What am I going to do with you*?"

Chapter 12

the real big bad

✶

"Looks like you've let the *vampire* cat out of the bag," Dr. Pamiver said. He shook his head, disappointed, then snatched the flashlight from Will's hand. He turned it off. "I guess we need to have a little talk now."

Will, Ivy, and Linus stood face-to-face with the head of the vampire army, Dr. Pamiver. A strange metal crown sat on his head, glowing red. Fitz growled as he stepped in front of Will. Nearby, a floating vampire cat hissed. The friends were surrounded on every side by hundreds of vampire animals.

Despite his pounding heart and shaking hands, Will was the first to act. He ripped the garlic chain from his neck and threw it at the veterinarian "Talk on this!"

Dr. Pamiver caught it in midair. He sniffed it. "Garlic? It's my favorite topping on a white pizza pie."

Ivy pulled the water gun from her belt, and took aim. "How about you wash it down with some holy water!"

Squirt-squirt.

Dr. Pamiver wiped his face, annoyed. "Seriously?"

Finally, Linus pulled out a giant silver cross and held it up. "This will strike fear in your heart!"

The vampire vet shook his head, pulling a necklace from inside his shirt. He was already wearing cross. "Really, children? I'm Catholic. I go to church every Sunday. Garlic, holy water, crosses—none of those work on real vampires. You can't believe everything you read on the internet."

The army of vampiric animals growled and hissed and clucked at the trio. The hovering swarm around them tightened, sealing off any hope of escape.

"We're screwed," Will said to the others. "I'm sorry I dragged you into this."

"You didn't drag us into anything," Ivy said. "It was our choice."

"It is not over yet." Linus fumbled something out of his fanny pack: a small homemade device. He whispered, "Will, Ivy, close your eyes on three. One…two…"

On "Three!" Linus threw the device. It exploded in an intense bright white flash so powerful that Will and Ivy could see from behind their closed eyelids. Linus shouted, "Run!"

With the vampires blinded, the three friends didn't hesitate—they ran. Will whistled, and Fitz flew after them. Dr. Pamiver screamed, his hands over his eyes. Still, he blocked the tunnel back to the vet's office. So they ran the opposite direction.

"What was that?!" Ivy shouted as she took the lead.

"A homemade flash grenade," Linus said. "A little chemistry experiment I cooked up, as a just-for-emergencies safety measure."

"You *made* that?" Ivy asked. "Respect, little brother!"

"It seems science does have its own merit in battling the supernatural."

"Where are we going?!" Will asked as they ran through the dark tunnels, lit only by two glow sticks.

"Anywhere that doesn't have vampires," Ivy snapped.

"These tunnels beneath East Emerson go on for miles," Linus stated. "We will be lost in no time, and those animals will find us by sense of smell alone. Our only option is to find a way out."

"Find them!" Dr. Pamiver's shout echoed through the tunnels, followed by the sound of hundreds of wings and screeches and nails against underground passages.

The three friends ran as hard as they could. Ivy had to continually slow down or wait for Linus and Will. She shook her head. "When this is over, you two have to start working out."

"My backpack...weighs...too much..." Linus wheezed.

Ivy yanked the bag off his back, tossing it to the side. Linus started to protest, but Ivy interrupted. "Leave it. Nothing in that pack is worth your life. Now run."

They came to a fork in the road, but a landslide blocked off one passageway. They turned left and kept going. They came to another fork and took another left. At the next fork, Ivy rushed to the right. The ground gave way under foot, and only Will's quick reactions saved her. He yanked her back, but she dropped her glow stick. The three watched as the glow stick fell and fell and fell—until it vanished.

"I owe you one," Ivy said, breathless.

"Just paying you back." Will smiled.

Linus took the garlic chains from his and his sister's

necks. He threw them into the ravine. "Perhaps the scent will mislead our trackers and buy us additional time."

"A brilliant mind with a brilliant scheme," said a familiar voice behind them. Will and Ivy saw the glowing fox behind them. *"'Tis wonderful to see you three working as a team. Now hurry. This way."*

Will and Fitz trailed behind the spirit animal, closely followed by Linus and Ivy. The fox navigated them through the various branches and splits in the labyrinth tunnels, and finally, up a spiraling stone staircase. At the top, the fox looked back at Will. *"You found the animals, now destroy the crown. You must shatter it to save the town."*

As the fox ran up the last steps, she dissipated into a swirl of fireflies, but not before illuminating a giant Roman numeral on the trapdoor:

VI

"Six," Will said. "Another door. Help me get it open."

Together, the three friends pushed against the heavy wooden door. It only gave way when Fitz joined their efforts. The trapdoor crashed open inside the chapel of an abandoned church. The pulpit was overturned, the pews scattered about. Bibles lay forgotten, their pages blowing under a breeze from the broken stained glass windows. Large stones from the floor had been cast about as though someone had been digging for gold. All of this shone in the moonlight, drifting in from the massive holes in the roof.

Will gazed around. A horrible feeling sunk in his chest. He couldn't explain it, but dread filled his lungs and chilled his blood. He was exhausted and terrified, but he remembered, he wasn't alone. He was with his friends, and somehow that was enough to give him strength.

"I'm in a church," Linus whispered, as he stepped into the remains of this sacred place. "Oracle Jones was right."

"Hurry!" Ivy cried, pulling her brother out of the tunnel. She and Will slammed the door shut behind him. The windows were too high to escape out of, and there only appeared to be one exit. The three friends ran toward the giant doors at the front of the church, but a giant fallen beam barred their way. The trio pushed and pulled, but it wouldn't give. Even when Fitz tried to use his vampire strength, the collapsed debris refused to budge.

"Use the pews," Will said. "We'll stack them and then climb out."

"Good idea," Ivy said.

As the team ran toward the nearest window, the trapdoor exploded into a thousand splinters. The vampire army had burst through. The swarm filled the church, swimming and spiraling into a circle overhead. Dr. Pamiver followed, floating up out of the hole. His arms were crossed in fury, and the crown on his head continued to radiate the darkest of reds. He scowled at our heroes. "Are you quite done running yet?"

"No! We'll go down fighting!" Will shouted. He grabbed a broken wooden plank from the ground, holding it up like a stake.

Dr. Pamiver's smirk fell into a frown. "*Fighting*? Why do humans always have to resort to violence? I only want to talk."

"Wait—" Will said, "*what?*"

Overhead, the animals barked and hissed and screeched.

"Shush, my sweet pets," Dr. Pamiver said softly. The crown glowed brighter, and all of the animals calmed. "I mean it. I only want to talk. Chat. Explain myself."

"Explain, then," Will cried. "Explain why you pet-napped all the animals in East Emerson and turned them into a vampire army!"

"Okay, I see how that could be misinterpreted," Pamiver said. "Let's press Pause, and everyone calm down for a minute. That includes you, my beauties."

The vampire veterinarian raised his hand, then lowered it. The crimson crown brightened, then dimmed, and every animal in the room stopped growling and relaxed. Animals of every shape and size, lowered from the air to take a seat—some settled on the rafters, others on broken pillars, the rest came all the way to the floor. Even Fitz lay down, submissive to the power of the crown.

"He's wearing the crown," Will whispered.

"You *just* noticed that?" Ivy asked.

"Where'd all these animals come from?" Linus asked, stunned. "Is that a cow in the rafters?"

"You can see them now that they're not flying," Ivy noted.

"They were flying?!" Linus asked, doubly surprised.

Pamiver walked to a nearby pew, and sat down. He looked tired as he buried his face into his hands. "How did everything go so wrong? I swear to you, I'm not a bad person."

"So...you're *not* going to *eat* us?"

"What? No! Of course not!" Pamiver was shocked by the accusation. "I fell in with a bad crew. I know that, but I'm using my powers for good—at least, for the good of animals. All I ever wanted was to protect them."

"Protect them from what?" Will asked.

"From pain," Pamiver whispered, "from death."

"Explain," Linus said.

"As a boy, my father was in the military. We moved around a lot. Every year, I found myself starting over, at a new school, surrounded by new people. And kids could be...cruel. The only friends I had were animals. My dog and my cat at first, but in new towns, I volunteered at vet offices and rescue shelters. Animals are innocent. They're not vicious and mean like people. I devoted my life to helping all creatures. I became a vet, a biology researcher, figuring out ways to help animals."

Will found himself feeling...not bad, but...he felt like he understood what Pamiver was saying. Moving, making new friends, having Fitz as the only constant in his life... Will's fear melted, changing into sympathy for Pamiver.

"Then last year I was approached by a woman who offered me proof of something I didn't think could possibly exist—*immortality*. And not just for me, for my animals. It seemed too good to be true. All she wanted was a favor when the time came. I honestly didn't know the full scope of her plan."

"'Her' who?" Ivy asked.

Pamiver gazed up, his face full of fear. "You wouldn't believe me if I told you."

"Try us."

"She's a witch. An ancient and powerful witch. Some say a goddess fallen from grace..."

"Tall, purple hair, conjures ghosts in cemeteries?" Will asked.

"You know Ozzie? Esther Oestre?"

"We know *of* her," Will said. A chill ran up his spine. "So you're part of The Thirteen?"

"Then you know," Pamiver said. He rushed forward, and got on his knees, grabbing Will's shirt, pleading. "I'm in over my head. When I joined, I thought she wanted to make the world a better place too. But I was wrong. Dead wrong."

"Are you crying?!" Ivy asked.

"*She killed me*. Literally. Do you know what that feels like?" Pamiver asked. "*Dying?* If she hadn't given me vampire blood, I would have…but she brought me back. Told me if I didn't do what she said, she'd make me suffer—for eternity. She told me to give my blood to the animals, build an army for her… She gave me this crown, it's some kind of magic relic, lets me communicate with the animals telepathically. She made me send the animals out, night after night, to feed off the locals. Draining them keeps them tired, weak…vulnerable—for the *next* step of her plan."

"Which is what?" Linus asked.

"I don't know everything. Everyone in The Thirteen has their own assignment that she gives us in code…"

Will's hand squeezed the golden pyramid in his pocket. But he knew better than to mention it. "If Ozzie is so powerful, why does she even need help?"

"Yeah," Ivy added. "Maybe she's not as powerful as you think."

"She… I don't…" Pamiver looked around, as if someone might be listening in the empty church. (If only, Cautious Reader, he had looked more closely. Then, he might have seen Faust, the Franken-hare, up in the rafters, watching the scene unfold…)

Pamiver leaned in, whispering, "I overheard some of

the others… Ozzie was a prisoner in Europe, locked up for the last century by witch-hunters. They drained her of magic. That's why she assembled The Thirteen, to help her, giving each of us a different task. I was meant to weaken the town, someone else to build an army of werewolves, a professor to dig out some kind of cave-in…"

"In the tunnels…" Will whispered. His head was so full that he couldn't see the big picture. What was Ozzie's plan? Before he could ask, Linus interrupted.

"Might I inquire why you are confessing everything to us?"

Pamiver sniffed, staining his cheeks with scarlet as he wiped away his tears. He stood. "I… I need to hypnotize you. Vampires can do that. I'll make you forget all of this. It's okay, it won't hurt. You'll go trick-or-treating, and… and you won't have to remember any of this."

Will stepped back, pulling Linus and Ivy with him. "If you're good, you have to help us. We have to stop her and The Thirteen."

"No," Dr. Pamiver said. "I have a plan. I'm leaving. Tonight. Me and the animals, we're going to escape. You three delayed me, but I don't want to hurt you, don't you see that? Let me just erase your memories, and you'll be free. You go your way, I'll go mine. You can be normal… live happy lives, until…*the end*."

Will thought of a few weeks ago. He wanted to take Mom and Fitz and leave too. But now? Now all he could think about were Ivy and Linus. About Ms. Delphyne, and even the chupacabra lunch lady. (Her tacos really were amazing.) Will couldn't just leave the town—not when everyone's life was in jeopardy. Will's sympathy for the vet vanished. "You're going to save yourself, and leave the rest of East Emerson to suffer and die?"

"What? No. I mean, yes, but I'm doing it for the animals," the vet argued. "Did you know the only animal species on the planet that knows hate is *humans*? Cats and dogs, horses and turtles—they don't know how to hate. They only know how to love. They deserve to inherit the earth."

"Why can't you help the animals *and* the people?" Ivy demanded.

"I can't," Pamiver said. "I can't go against Ozzie and the others. I'm too weak."

"We're only kids, and we're doing it. And you're a frigging vampire! You have to at least try!"

"No," Pamiver said. "I'm leaving with the animals tonight. You can't change my mind."

"Then you *are* a bad guy," Will said.

"I am not!" Pamiver growled. "Enough of this. Come here. It's time to forget." When Pamiver made a grab for Will, Fitz attacked the vampire's hand. Fitz refused to let go, even as the vet screamed.

Pamiver kicked Fitz away. "Bad dog! You're not obedient yet. But you will be!" The crown on his head began to glow, making Fitz back away and tuck his tail. The dog whimpered, as if Pamiver were hurting him.

"Stop it!" Will cried.

"Then come here," Pamiver growled.

"Fine," Will said. "Just answer one question first. *Why* is Ozzie doing all of this?"

Dr. Pamiver almost laughed. "Why does anyone do anything? For love. She's trying to resurrect Simon—"

Suddenly, the vet gasped for air. His face started to turn red, as though he couldn't breathe. Pamiver grabbed at his own neck, pulling at it, as though something invisible were choking him.

"That's quite enough talking from you," said a voice from above.

Through the largest hole in the roof, Ozzie floated downward as if on a breeze. All of the animals whined and hissed, backing away in absolute fear. Except for Franken-Hare, with its cybernetic eye and dragon wings, as it flew down and perched on her shoulder, nestling its face in the witch's purple hair.

Ozzie's feet never touched the church floor, levitating just a few inches above it. The hare hissed, like a cat, at Fitz. Will's dog snarled back.

"Mistress Ozzie!" Dr. Pamiver begged. He dropped to his knees and bowed his head. "This…this isn't what it looks like!"

"No?" Ozzie said, surveying Will, Ivy, Linus. She raised her hand to rub the hare's ear. "Because it sounded like you've been revealing my secrets to a bunch of children."

"I can explain—" Dr. Pamiver pleaded.

"The time for explanations is done—as is your time as my servant," Ozzie said. The witch raised her hands and they began to crackle with electricity and arcane energy. A wind from nowhere circled her, blowing Will, Ivy, Linus, and Fitz backward.

Oestre said, almost gently, with a vicious smile: *"Yad*

otni thgin nrut nus tel, traeh sih dnif thgil tel. Yal eh erehw enihs noom eht tel, Trap sduolc eht tel."

Through some horrible magic, moonlight began to gather into a beam. The blinding ray shot through the open ceiling, becoming brighter and stronger until it shone as bright as day.

"No, please!" the vet begged.

The sunbeam lit upon Dr. Pamiver. His soul-shaking cries resounded throughout the building as he burst into flame and crumbled to dust. As the dust drifted down like snow, the crimson crown crashed with a *CLANK!* against the stone floor. The sunlight faded and the moon became itself again. Night returned, as if nothing horrible, horrific, and horrifying had happened at all.

Then it began to snow. It was cool, but not cold. It was only October 31, yet it was snowing. As if nature demanded a balance after Ozzie's strange magic. Will might have thought it beautiful, it might have reminded him of winter holidays in New York, if he hadn't just seen someone murdered. He could hear nothing except the cold silence of air as it tried to hold on to the echoes of Dr. Pamiver's final screams.

"Murderer!" he shouted. He rushed forward, racing

up an inclined pew, and leaped at her, ready to tackle her with nothing but his fists.

Ozzie raised her hand, catching him midair in an invisible grip. He floated there, unable to move. "You thought to hurt me with what? Your mortal fists?"

"Of course not." Will smiled. "I'm just the distraction."

On the floor, Ivy held the crimson crown—and Linus's ax. She raised it up.

Too late, Ozzie screamed, "No!"

Ivy brought the ax down, shattering the crown into thousands of glass shards. A blast of crimson energy burst from it, tossing everyone back several feet. The crown fragments began to melt, turning to blood.

The swarms of vampire animals began to float down from above, like balloons losing their helium. Fangs retracted, shrinking into normal teeth. The red glow in their eyes dimmed until they were normal. Fitz lost his ability to fly, as his four paws touched the ground again. The last of the animals drifted to the floor like snowflakes. As soon as they landed, they scurried to the corners of the church, as if instinctively terrified of the witch.

"Foolish brats! Do you know what you've cost me?!"

Ozzie threw Will across the room with a gesture. He crashed into Ivy and Linus.

Ozzie floated toward them, tattooed fingers curling into fists. She punched a nearby pillar with her fist, shattering it. The whole building shook as parts of the ceiling caved in.

Will, Ivy, and Linus ran toward the nearest broken window. They were almost there when the witch commanded, *"Evom ton od."*

Instantly, the trio froze in place, as still as ice statues. *"Em ecaf dna nrut,"* Oestre said. All three twisted to face the witch.

Fitz snarled and barked, running in front of the children to protect them.

"Ecnelis," Oestre said. Fitz's bark muted.

Franken-Hare leaped from her shoulder and landed in front of Fitz, hissing again. Fitz backed away.

It was just Ozzie and the three friends. Ozzie paced in a full circle around them. "You are but children. Of course. Ever the witch's plight. What should I do with them, Faust? Turn them into frogs? Make a cake with their bones? Boil them alive? So many choices."

Faust's hare nose and whiskers flexed.

"Oh, my! Now that's a clever idea," Ozzie snarled. "You've decimated the first part of my plan. You've cost me a disciple. And you've ruined All Hallow's Eve for me, when I should be in the forest, gathering strength from the spirits. I should slaughter all three of you..."

Ozzie grabbed Will by the throat. Unable to move, he could only wince as her fingers tightened. A sinister smile crawled across Ozzie's face as she squeezed...

Though they could not move, Dear Reader, Will, Ivy, and Linus were shaking—not only in their flesh, but in their hearts. They knew East Emerson was weird, and they knew they were in for an adventure, but they had not known how far it would go. Certainly, Oracle Jones had warned them, and they had heard her words, but had they truly understood? Darling Reader, I'm afraid it's difficult for any youth to fully comprehend when an adult warns them about danger. You think you might know better, but you often do not. Our heroes certainly didn't. And now? Now they were faced with the cost of their choices...which might cost them their lives.

Their thoughts raced. They wondered if their parents might appear with a cadre of police or army soldiers. Or perhaps the silver fox would arrive to save them. Or maybe

Oracle Jones and her lemur Gumbo Jones would swoop in on a broom and battle the purple-haired enchantress. Some part of Will hoped his dad would suddenly appear and save the day.

None of those things happened.

They were on their own. And they were helpless.

They thought of their families, their friends, and the things they had meant to do, but hadn't.

Will felt an intense amount of guilt for bringing Linus and Ivy and Fitz into this. He also felt guilty for how he had treated his mom, how he reacted to their "fresh start." He promised himself, if he made it through this, he would make amends.

Linus also felt an intense amount of guilt. He considered himself a man of science and preparedness. He thought he'd brought all they would need. But he was wrong. And now there was nothing he could do.

Ivy also felt guilt. She hadn't yet achieved her life goals of eating an entire cake in one sitting, or watching twenty-four hours of television straight without sleep, or becoming stinking-rich and famous. She also hadn't told Linus or her parents just how much she loved and appreciated them.

Dear Reader, you might feel your own heart ache for our heroes in this moment. You might worry they are about to die. You might worry you read this entire wretched book only to watch three somewhat-likable protagonists be slaughtered by a witch.

I did warn you ahead of time. This is *not* a happy story. But if you are feeling these things, be grateful. That means you have a heart, and are not a monster like me.

Will closed his eyes, as he felt Ozzie's fingers crushing his windpipe. Despite the power of the magic holding him, Will pushed with all of his strength—and somehow managed to take Ivy's hand in his left, and Linus's with his right. He was scared, and he knew they were too.

"I'm sorry," he whispered. "Whatever happens now, I'm glad I met you both."

"Likewise," said Linus.

"Ditto," Ivy added.

"Enough," Ozzie said, her eyes crackling with electricity, her fingers tingling with lightning. "Say goodbye—"

"WAIT!"

The three friends couldn't move to turn their heads. But Will recognized the guttural timbre before the bearded gray-skinned man stepped into view. The stranger jumped down from one of the windows. (Cherished Readers, this is what we call a last-minute twist. You're welcome.)

He walked over slowly, his hand raised to Ozzie. "THERE IS NO NEED TO KILL THEM."

"Isn't there?" she asked, gnashing her teeth.

"YOU NEED THEM ALIVE, " he said, "FOR NOW."

The witch released Will's neck. She stepped back, not releasing her gaze from Will's face.

"MAKE THEM FORGET, OZZIE. LET THEM GO. WHEN THE TIME COMES, YOU'LL NEED THEM. YOU'LL NEED EVERYONE IN THIS TOWN."

"*Humph*," Ozzie groaned. With her finger, she tapped Will's, Ivy's, and Linus's noses in succession, as if a grandmother passing out kisses. "It's true. We require your *blood*, your *fear*, and your *souls*. Each of you belongs to East Emerson, and East Emerson? *It belongs to Simon and his serpent*."

The sorceress waved her fingers over them and chanted, "*Nees ev'uoy srorroh eht gnieesnu, tegrof lliw sdnim ruoy, neeb ev'uoy secalp eht gniwonknu, tegrof lliw sdnim ruoy. Wons s'retniw tsal ekil sdnim ruoy morf enog, wonk ton lliw uoy ecaf ym.*"

Will felt the black tourmaline charm burn against his chest, as though it were absorbing the spell. Oracle had been right, about everything, including this. Only, Linus had lost his. . . .

"Now," Ozzie said. "Go home. Go to sleep. Remember none of this."

With a swish of her hand, the three friends could move now. As if in a trance, Linus blinked sleepily. "I will go home, I will go to sleep, and I will remember none of this."

Before he released it, Will squeezed Ivy's hand. She understood. Playing along, Ivy and Will repeated after Linus, "I will go home, I will go to sleep, and I will remember none of this."

Linus led the way toward the lowest window. Ivy followed. And Will followed her. Though he knew he shouldn't, he couldn't stop himself from looking at the gray-skinned stranger. He'd saved them again. But he worked with Ozzie. Who was he? And what did he want?

The stranger's eyes met the ground as he bowed before the witch. "YOUR ORDERS?"

"Begin the November phase," Ozzie said as she floated up into the sky, her Franken-hare flying after her. "Notify the rest of The Thirteen."

Just before she flew away, she looked back at the

bearded man and called out, "What you did for those children was kind… Don't do it again. The end is coming, whether you like it or not."

Chapter 13

~~The End~~ Not the End

✷

When Will got home, it was nearly midnight. Halloween, and October with it, would be over in a few minutes.

As soon as he walked through the door, Mom grabbed him by both arms. She looked at him, covered in dirt and filth, looking as if he'd been through an obstacle course, or maybe a war. Then she pulled him into a deep, strong hug. "Where have you been?! I was worried sick!"

Fitz rushed in behind Will, barking and wagging his tail.

"I found my dog," Will said.

"Where—? How—?" Ms. Vásquez started and stopped. She hugged Will again. "It doesn't matter.

Are you okay? What happened to your neck? It looks bruised."

Will didn't want to lie to his mom, but he also knew he couldn't tell her the whole truth. Instead, he just told her *some* of the truth: "I got a little banged up, I'm fine. I was with Ivy and Linus all night, trick-or-treating, saving the town, trying to find Fitz, that sort of stuff. I guess we lost track of time. I'm really sorry. Not just for being late tonight, but for everything. I know I've been difficult since we moved here, but I think I was just… I don't know…scared. But I shouldn't be scared. I have you. I have Fitz. I even have friends. I'm sorry. I'm really, honestly, sorry."

Ms. Vásquez looked at Will, tears welling in her eyes. She hugged Will one more time, then hugged Fitz too. "Thank you for saying all of that. I'm so glad you're all right. Both of you. And I'm glad you're making friends, even if they should have known better than to stay out so late."

"Am I in trouble?" Will asked.

Ms. Vásquez hesitated. Then she smiled. "I think we can let it slide—but just this once. Okay?"

Will nodded.

"Now, get upstairs, brush your teeth, and go to bed. It is way past your bedtime." Ms. Vásquez sighed a heavy sigh. "Oh, and, Will?"

"Yeah, Mom?"

"Did you have fun tonight?"

Will didn't know how to answer that. He'd had the adventure of a lifetime. He'd found the missing animals. He'd saved the town. And he'd faced an evil witch and lived to tell the tale. Plus, he'd made two friends.

"Yeah, I guess I did."

Will started up the stairs, then stopped. He raced back and threw his arms around his mom. He hugged her for a long time.

He didn't know how to tell her that they might be doomed.

When Will got to his room, he crawled into bed with Fitz. But he wasn't tired. In fact, he was wide-awake. He recalled the golden pyramid and Dr. Pamiver's scroll in his pants pocket. He grabbed a pen and began to decipher the text.

P=A MIVER,

VXL WIL OEBBM.

WVY(RBVY P(HDPEX H(WB P(PYDR.

VXL WIL NYBT(WB NB(WYBE WILD.

IPUL WILD KLLM B(WIL NHWHQL(X BK LPXW LDLYXB(.

WBJLWILY, WIL 13 THEE KH(M XHDB('X OBMR P(M XBVE.

TL THEE OYH(J IHD OPNF

WB KLLM B(WIL XLYAL(W.

WIL(WIL TBYEM THEE KPEE.

—BLXWYL

He used the cipher, matching *A* with *Z*, *B* with *Y*, *C* with *X*, and so on…only it *didn't* work. Will didn't understand. It had worked before in the tunnels. Why not now?

He studied the scroll again…when he first read it, he thought the "=" between the *P* and *A* was a mistake. What if it wasn't?

He examined the golden pyramid, turning it over and over. In frustration he squeezed it. *CLICK*. Slowly releasing his hold, the second ring of the cipher jumped a spot. He whispered, "It *moves*."

He pressed it again, then turned the inner wheel counterclockwise, twisting the hidden mechanism until the *P* matched up with the *A*.

He tried decoding the scroll now. After he deciphered the first line, he realized it worked. He had just finished decoding the whole thing when Linus's walkie-talkie went off. "Come in, Will. Do you read me?"

"I don't read you, but I can hear you," Will whispered into the receiver as he walked to his window. He peered outside and across the street. Ivy and Linus waved.

"We can't sleep," Ivy said.

"Me either," Will said. "And I just discovered something else." He told them about the golden pyramid, about the scroll, about the cipher. He read it to them. "My mind is spinning. I have so many questions."

"So do I. So does Linus," Ivy said. She shared the walkie with her brother.

Linus said, "The witch took my memories."

"Wait. So how—"

"Do I remember tonight? I don't. But Ivy told me everything."

"And you believe her?"

Linus grinned. "I am a man of science. I believe what I learn through my senses—which is why I had an audio recorder with me the entire evening. Being overly prepared and paranoid comes in handy when documenting conversations with villainous vampires and wicked witches who can erase memories. Now I have auditory proof that what you and Ivy have been saying is true—this town is indeed made up of magic, monsters, myths, and mad science."

Ivy added, "Yup. So I guess the questions is, what is our little Supernatural Society going to do about it?"

Will pointed to the black asphalt street between their houses. The moonlit fox stood there, smiling at Ivy and Linus before turning to Will. She ran, transformed into a silver kestrel, and flew up to Will's windowsill. Before Will could say a word, she spoke. *"Beware the full moon and hirsute strangers. East Emerson is still full of dangers."*

Will spoke into the walkie. "Did you hear that?"

"Loud and clear," Ivy said.

"I heard nothing except the chirp of a bird," Linus said, annoyed.

Ivy laughed. "Will, ask that fox if she can score my brother a magic ring or something."

"Well?" Will asked.

The kestrel smiled. *"I'll see what I can do. But you need to be ready to save the town—again."*

"I'm already ready," Will said. "Where do we start?"

a temporary farewell

My Dearest, Dreadful, Doomed Reader,

You survived reading this book!

I cannot tell you how much it warms my cold, barely beating heart to know that you still draw breath. I was worried. You see, the first few friends I sent this book to must have perished upon reading it because I never heard back from any of them. I assumed that anyone who read it might die–which is why I tried to warn you *NOT* to read this book.

Well...that...and...if I'm, being 100% truly honest... I may...possibly...have been a little...eetsy teensy tiny bit...*afraid*...that you wouldn't like my story. And that would be worse than if you had died!

If you hated it, I would have been devastated. And what's worse than an insecure monster with anger issues and a lot of internal rage? But let us not focus on that, because you loved it, right? RIGHT?

Good. Let's move on.

I am so proud. You were brave, you persevered, and you ignored me. As you should have! After all, I am a monster. Monster advice is monstrous advice. Do not heed it. You didn't, you read, and yet you live! Congratulations. You survived.

Didn't you?

Sincerely, and worst,

yours darkly,

-Adam Monster

P.S.

My story is not over.

Neither is Will's.

Or Linus's.

Or Ivy's.

But I beg of you. Do NOT read the next book.

It will come at a terrible cost. My next narrative will no doubt cause nightmares, nasty nausea, nervousness, negative notions, necromancer incantations, and possibly diarrhea. No one wants that.

What do you mean, YOU DO?!

Sigh.

Of course you do. I suspected as much. See you soon then, human child. Until next time...sleep tight, I hope the bed bugs bite.

p.p.s.

Ia wbacsd geofignhgi tjok wlrmintoep yqorus at suevcwrxeytz maëbscsdaegfe, bguhti hjoknlemsntolpyq, Ir'ms mtuucvhw txoyoz taïbrcedde.

Wfhgahti? Djoknl'tm gneotp aqnrgsrtyu wviwtxhy mzea.

Wbrcidteifnggh ai bjokolkm inso ap lqorts otfu wvowrxky.

Wzraïbtcidnegf ag bhoiojkk wlimtnho speqcrrsettu cvowdxeysz?

Eavbecnd meofrgeh sioj.

Tkillm nneoxptq trismteu!

*****